Vicki Hendricks is the author of noir novels *Miami Purity* and *Iguana Love*. She lives in Hollywood, Florida, and teaches writing at Broward Community College.

**Also by Vicki Hendricks
and published by Serpent's Tail**

Iguana Love

The verdict on *Iguana Love*

'In stretching noir's sexual borders so far, beating at the boundaries of gender in a style of deceptive intelligence and disconcerting wit, Hendricks has achieved something important and new ... The dead diviners of noir's masculine psyche – Chandler, Hammett and Cain – might be shocked at such manoeuvres. But Hendricks is their first true female equivalent'
Independent on Sunday

'If James M Cain were a woman and alive today, the postman would only ring once on the doors of the sultry Miami condos inhabited by Hendricks' characters in heat. Guaranteed to raise your temperature, whatever the weather'
Guardian

'A guilty pleasure to savour slowly'
Time Out

'Part thriller, part porn, part redneck comedy, *Iguana Love* is gleefully immoral, a style that relishes its own perversity and is seductive in its brutality'
Arena

voluntary madness

◆◆◆◆◆◆◆◆◆◆◆◆◆◆◆◆◆◆◆◆

vicki hendricks

Library of Congress Catalog Card Number: 00–102181

A catalogue record for this book is available from the
British Library on request

The right of Vicki Hendricks to be identified as the author
of this work has been asserted by her in accordance with
the Copyright, Designs and Patents Act 1988

First published in 2000 by Serpent's Tail,
4 Blackstock Mews, London N4 9NT

Website: www.serpentstail.com

Phototypeset by Intype London Ltd
Printed in Great Britain by Mackays of Chatham, plc

10 9 8 7 6 5 4 3 2 1

To
Chuck Eisman
(1948–1996)

Acknowledgements

A "millennium" of thanks to my publisher Pete Ayrton; my editor, John Williams; and all the Serpent's Tail staff.

Thanks to the "living legends" of Key West, some of whom inspired fictional scenes in the story. These are the keepers of the flame, preserving the bohemian character of the city despite the threat of family entertainment and t-shirt shops. And thanks to all the restaurant owners and chefs of the lower keys who allowed me into the corners of their kitchens to observe and sketch the layout. Also, thanks to Detective Sergeant E.J Yannacone, who schooled me on Key West Police procedure and the law. Hope I got it right!

Finally, thanks to my friend Woody for his support and friendship, and as an inspiration for more than one character in my writing.

In tribute to the city and people I love, the names and places used here are often real, but the scenes involving them are pure fiction.

*It is a fearful thing to love
what death can touch.*

— **Anonymous, from a gravestone**

1

◆◆◆◆◆◆◆◆◆◆◆◆◆◆◆◆◆

Across the bar a lean blond with a missing front tooth is massaging my tits with his eyes, and I get an idea. I'm on my third margarita at Viva Zapata in Key West, bored with the chit-chat on both sides. It's one of those nights when my sweetie – Punch – is at Captain Tony's drinking with his budds, knowing whatever I do, I'm thinking of him. It's true – his hard muscles with the smoothest Kahlua and cream skin, thick black hair past his shoulders, a view of the world evolved way past our time – I'm his, body and soul, no regrets, till I die – promised seven months from now, at the end of October.

A creative scene is forming in my head, and I have to try it. That's a personal vow, since my twenty-second birthday. After Pop died, I got sick of weighing and choosing my options when nothing turned out to be in my hands from the start. Now I challenge the insanity of life with my crazy mind. That way there's no judgment and no expectations – except for, like, gravity – and lots of surprises.

What I need is material for Punch's life's work, his novel, to make it exciting. The book's the only thing that matters to both of us. All I ever did was work at Cracker Barrel restaurant –

besides being Pop's full-time housekeeper – but I always wanted
to be a writer. We read about Hemingway in high school, and I'd
be an adventurer-novelist myself, if I had the brains – which I
don't. I know my limitations. So being with Punch is the next
best thing, the only thing for me.

I'm ready to get some cool night air on my hot moist skin
when Blondie comes up. He's shouting against the loud hard
rock, something about us having leeway since we're both blonds.
I nod, whether I'm hearing right or not. He asks my name and I
tell him Juliette.

"Romeo," he says, and points to himself grinning. He seems
like a nice guy, but far gone.

"Got one already," I tell him.

He starts talking and I pick up a bit about his co-workers in
construction. One time they made him a replacement tooth out
of epoxy. I'm supposed to be impressed. I am. I picture the kelly
green peg of hardened glue set next to the other teeth.

"So where is it?" I ask.

He laughs and sticks his finger in the gap. "Won't stay put."

I laugh with him, but I'm thinking of my mother and her
lover. He had a front tooth missing. His bridge was found broken
on the floor, next to her bloody nude body. I wasn't supposed to
hear the story – I was just a kid. But knowing the cruel truth
about life like that is what makes me feel I should be a writer.

I finish the last gulp of margarita number three and pick my
dollars off the bar. Moving away, I yell "Bye," and put my hand
up in a sort of wave-and-halt signal, so he doesn't follow me out.
He mouths, "Bye, Juliette," with a sad look on his face.

Three drinks are my limit, what I call a drinking session.
More than that and I forget stuff or go inside myself. I want to
be conscious, not lose details or feelings. Punch and me set ourselves a year to play with and it's half gone already. Soon it'll be
lights out, tits up – R.I.P., motherfuckers.

I've been thinking a lot about death – I'm not all that keen

on it. But I can do what I have to, if the time comes. I gave it a
go once, but Pop had my stomach pumped.

This time I'll eat the sleeping pills with Punch. On our last
night we'll get our bodies air-brushed to look like skeletons and
ride Captain Tony's float in the Fantasy Fest Parade. Right in
front of Sloppy Joe's we'll make a big toast and swallow the
pills. Everybody will think we're just drunk until it's too late.
Thousands of people will see our dead bodies curled up together
and laugh at how we're partied out. Then we'll be the highlight
on the news and they'll see what kind of party it was, how much
the surface differs from the truth, as Punch would say. I've known
that all my life with Pop, but never said it out loud. Yeah, irony
hits hard, Punch says.

But if Punch writes his Great American Novel, I'm figuring
he'll want to live. He'll be happy forever and won't have to drink
himself into a coma anymore. That'll improve his health a lot,
keep his blood sugar more stable. We can have a real life together.
Being with Punch is the only dream I ever had. I'll do fucking
anything for him. When I think for one second how he tried to
take care of his mother, my eyes water up – if only I could go
back in time and make it all better. He was twelve when she died
– cancer, his grandpa told him later on – but for years he thought
she starved because he didn't bring her enough healthy food.
They were living alone in some downtown room when she got
bad, and he had to steal for both of them. I think some old men
might have used him too, but there's no sense dwelling on that.
He didn't tell anybody his mother died for four or five days. He
kept piling up food the whole time, and then he just took off. I
don't want to think about it.

I turn left toward Catherine Street, more like an alley, which
is why I choose it. When the beat throbs down behind me, the
night's quiet. The black sky is silver-glittered above the yellow
glow of the street. It's probably near two. I'm light with tropical
abandon – ready to screw with convention.

The breeze blows clear through my short rayon dress. It's short and loose – like me, until I met Punch. I wear thong panties because I like them better than none. Punch likes them too. The stretch nylon rides the taper of my waist above my hips, makes my skinny ass look round. The grip is firm between my legs. When a breeze flares out my skirt I get wet with knowing how good I look. I can almost fly.

I head left up Catherine Street a couple blocks to a stone wall in the shadow of Australian pines. I know the spot. It's on the way home, but I'm not ready to go home. Punch and I try to make interesting things happen for the book – create truth that's stranger than fiction. My idea is for a racy scene. I hope it works well enough for Punch to use it.

I slip off my thong and sit down on the rock wall to wait for some company. I think of my mother who's been dead since I was nine. She'd left Pop and taken off for California. I think she was happier there, right up to the fatal beating. I remember the guy. He killed her right after I made my one visit.

My ass is pressed into crumbly stone and long, soft pine needles. They imbed my cheeks. This should be a comedy scene. Somebody might say it's tragic, I guess, my whole damn life – but not me. I know exactly what I'm doing and why. I take a joint out of my bag and light it up.

I let a couple pass me. Then a young man. He's dark, maybe Bahamian, too hip. I know from his walk I'd never catch him off guard.

After a few hits, I put the joint out and finger myself while I wait, feel the tingle. I wish Punch was lurking in the shadows to watch. I can't wait to tell him what I'm doing. Maybe he'll take notes. I hold my little tits through the rayon, like he does, and pinch the nipples, one then the other to make them stick out. I relight the joint, suck on it, hold the smoke. I picture the shining need Punch gets in his eyes. He says something supernatural happens when he looks at me.

I see the one I want passing under the light. He looks hurried, needs slowing down. Tall and gawky, tidy hair, shorts, t-shirt and sneakers. Closer up, I figure late twenties, a tourist sunburn. Nice guy. Probably thinks all girls are like his sister. I put down the joint, whip off my dress, and step out in front of him.

He flinches. His eyes take hold, my tits, my crotch.

I throw my head back, my arms straight up, with hands curved like a ballerina.

He shakes his head, trying to unscramble his thoughts. He backs off.

I step forward, close in till my nipples touch his t-shirt. I stare at his eyes, raccoon-mask sunburn.

"What do you want?" he says.

I smell beer on his breath, hope it hasn't given him too much courage. "Surprise me," I say. My voice sounds husky, like Kathleen Turner I think.

He takes a giant step back, laughs. It's a nervous laugh, like I'm counting on.

"Come here," I say. I'm chuckling, trying to hold back the giggles the weed is bubbling up in my chest.

He stares. He looks around. "I gotta go. I don't need any trouble."

"There's nobody in the bushes."

He looks both ways.

I glance around. We're still alone. I whisper, "You think this is candid camera? It's not. Believe me."

I take his hand to my hair, then turn my face and lick his palm, laugh.

He stiffens, looks both ways again. "I bet you have AIDS or something."

"Doubt it." I shrug. My nipples rub up and down on his T-shirt. I want to tell him I'm working on a novel, but that would spoil it.

He frowns and his lips go out. He's younger than I thought.

His voice is bold. "I heard of a woman like that," he says. "She writes it the morning after – with lipstick on the mirror – 'You've got AIDS.' "

"I heard that. I bet it's made up."

He's thinking.

I'm wondering where to go with this. No way I'm going to fuck him. I should've made more of a plan. "Hey, take off, buddy," I say. "You just got flashed, that's all. Go tell your girlfriend. You were good – didn't hardly look."

His lips scrunch to the side, like he's not too happy about being good, but he nods and sidesteps away.

I laugh. "Hey," I holler. "Now you've got a Key West story for your friends back home in Indiana."

The guy turns. From the look on his face, I think I guessed right. I walk into a patch of light, smile and wave. I think next time I should bring a gun – just for effect. Since I thought it, now I have to do it. I giggle. Picture little me holding a gun. Punch will like that for the book. Too bad my mother didn't have a gun. I might have gotten to know her better.

2

◆◆◆◆◆◆◆◆◆◆◆◆◆◆◆◆◆◆

I slip my dress on, then burn my finger relighting the joint for the walk home. I have six or seven blocks to Watson Street where Punch and I rent a cottage in a compound. That's what they call these walled-in clusters of houses in Key West. Sounds like a prison, but hell no, just the opposite. There are eight small cottages inside, with a pool in the middle. The walls protect us from normal people and routine. I can swim topless in broad daylight and nude at night. Nobody cares, gay or straight. Only the cats bother to watch.

I walk by my car in the small parking lot and stop at our high wooden gate. We have a buzzer on the inside to let in guests if we had any. It's my own private world with Punch. I open the gate with my key and walk under the trees. There's an aroma of night-blooming jasmine tinged with cat urine. It's not a bad smell, kind of sexual. I remember the night Punch brought gardenias inside. He'd spilled rum, and the two smells mixed – peppery honey. I wanted to suck it all in, it was so delicious. I told Punch they should make men's cologne like that. "Eau de Punch," he said. Simple as that. I look up at those long dark lashes and I have to love him.

I sit on a porch chair to finish the joint, listen to Punch snoring inside. I glance through the window. The light's on and he's slumped in the big rattan chair. It's good. He's asleep – not in a diabetic coma, which is always a possibility if he forgot to eat. I know he's wearing his contacts. They're hard ones and he'll be aggravated in the morning with his burning eyes.

I toss the roach into an ashtray and go inside to rouse him. It's dangerous. His arms usually fling out like he's under attack. I crouch and cup my hand on the back of his head, give a short massage into his scalp under the long black hair. He's still gorgeous – unwrinkled face except for a few lines around the eyes that give away his deep-down kindness, iron streaks over his temples showing strength. His father being Jamaican and his mother Italian must have been a strange combo those days in Tennessee. Maybe that's why he's called Punch, from defending himself on all sides. Looking close I can see a couple scars, one a short crease above the middle of his upper lip. I don't know about any of them. I never asked. I have enough painful details already.

He moves. I jerk backwards and land my ass on the wood floor. I rub my left cheek and feel silly. I laugh, but it doesn't wake him.

My vow to stay with Punch was the first important step in my life. We were broken up for months. Because Punch is much older and looks black, my father tried to keep us apart. He never saw Punch's intelligence or understood his suffering – or the way he loves me. Pop couldn't appreciate a writer's sensitivity and the part of me that lives off Punch's creative mind. He said Punch was a no-count bum, and I'd end up like my mother. I got used to hearing that. "You can't save the whole world," he'd say. "I know," I'd tell him. "I'm not interested in the whole world."

I look at Punch's open mouth. His drinking didn't go over with Pop either. Punch hurt me once, but he didn't mean it. I hit him first, and he was just trying to hold me back. After that he almost left me, so it would never happen again. I couldn't let him go.

When Pop died, our house and all the contents went to the Presbyterian Church, his congregation. I got insurance money, and practically everybody tried to take me home for a while, but I couldn't live with strangers. That's what they were – even in such a small country town. My way was clear and I made my decision to be with Punch. I'll love him forever.

I knew it since the first day we met at the Seven-Eleven. He was passing through Fort Pierce on his way to Miami that morning and decided to stay, just for me. I saved him – he told me later. Until he saw me, he was planning to rob that store – he'd got that desperate, to the point he thought the whole world owed him something and he was gonna get some of it. But one look at those big eyes of mine, he says, and he couldn't take a chance on me getting hurt.

I'd found out his plan – by accident. I was fixing a coffee for myself, and I accidentally brushed back his jacket and saw the gun. I looked up at him and slopped my coffee on the floor. I never saw a man so beautiful. I was hypnotized by his smoothness and the danger. I could read the whole thing on his face. I told him I worked at Cracker Barrel, right by the turnpike, and if he stopped in later – without his gun – I'd buy him dinner.

That night he had chicken and dumplings, mashed potatoes, turnip greens, and for dessert, a chocolate cobbler with vanilla ice cream. He drank a lot of iced tea so I had to keep coming back to refill his glass. Each time, he'd take my hand and feed me bites of cobbler, tell me how beautiful I was, caress my cheek. He said I was an angel, and he was afraid I might disappear. He treated me like a princess. I couldn't wait to get my clunky uniform off and feel his warm smooth hands on my naked skin. We never slept that night. He paid attention to every part of my body and my mind. We told secrets and fell in love, a kind of love nobody has the right to end. I never saw the gun again.

I got the idea for us to live in Key West on my inheritance. Punch got a gig playing guitar with a band for a couple months until my money was settled and he sold his car and threw that in. Punch is a wonderful musician. He traveled all over Europe playing on the street when he was young. He planned to play Key West, but it isn't worth his time. The place is overrun. I told him he didn't have to work. Back then the sixty-two thousand dollars we put together seemed an impossible amount to spend in one year.

It was Punch's idea to write his book about us. All he ever wanted to do in his life was write a novel. Hemingway was always his idol. I told him he's a genius and owes it to the world. He said the only thing to do was to take control of his fate – write the novel and end his life before everything turned to shit, meaning his health because of the drinking and diabetes. He's forty-four and has quit trying to control the booze. Me, I can't see any reason to live without Punch. I never had a life till he came along, and I'm not going back to that loneliness. No more to it. Promised together forever.

We started our year last October, so we'll end it at Fantasy Fest on Halloween night – make it the grand-finale party of our lives. We figured the money out exactly, rent plus $150 to share a day, to live as wild as we can, eating and drinking and carousing, and use it all up – on most anything we want, except cocaine. Punch and I agree that freedom still has boundaries, but if you're smart enough, you can choose them yourself.

We've got a one-year guarantee never to get bored – because we know it's our last. You can do a hell of a lot if you don't worry about the future or fear death. "Nothing's right or wrong, good or bad," Punch says, "just more or less interesting."

I stand behind his chair where he can't reach me and touch his shoulder. He's still sound asleep. I stare at his long lashes. It takes at least two minutes of poking and rubbing until he finally moves.

His eyes open. His left arm chops to the side like he's hitting something away from his face. "Fuck, shit," he yells.

I know he's not mad at me. He's just out of it. "Honey, what's the matter?" I say.

"Fuck, 's all fucked. Fucking . . . fucking assholes . . ."

I stroke Punch's cheek. "Why don't you get your contacts out?" I try to hoist him out of the chair by nudging myself under his armpit, knowing it's impossible. He's six-two, two-hundred pounds, so even though I'm strong for my size, at five-three, one-hundred-five, I'd need a crane to budge him.

Finally he takes the hint. "Sorry, sorry," he mumbles. He pokes his head toward me for a kiss, but misses. I move close so he can get me. Sweet rum. He pulls himself up and heads to the bathroom, grabbing the wall to steady himself. I follow, in case I can help. I don't say anything because it's better not to.

He holds the plastic contact case an inch from his eyes, squirts the solution so hard it sizzles into the tiny cups. One by one he manages to get his contacts in there. He's legally blind without lenses, but can see real close up.

He puts on his thick glasses and rocks past me before I can move away from the door. I follow him and pull off my dress and panties and drop them next to his jeans. When I crawl into bed he rolls close to me on his side and takes my arm across his neck. His eyes are closed, but he kisses my hand, then starts to snore lightly. I fit myself spoon-style around his smooth firm ass, with my face against his warm back. It's April so the nights are still cool, but his body heat is all I need.

I open my eyes and it's the morning of a great day. I have a quirky idea all ready for us. I look down and Punch looks up at me from between my thighs. He's just ready to dip with his tongue. "Mornin', babycakes," he says. His eyebrows go up and he gives me that wicked smile. I know it's going to be a good day. I open my thighs further and lay my legs over his back. He roots his face down into me and I get juicy. His tongue is as rhythmic as a dog's and he's as untiring.

Something I love about Punch, he's not squeamish. He adores every part of me. He'd go down on me with my period, if I let him.

I feel myself clenching. I want his big, hard cock inside me, but I know it's not going to happen. I let go, ride the waves of coming. My chin goes up and I feel my eyes roll back into a deeper level of the universe.

When I open my eyes, Punch is out of bed pulling on his jeans. I see his empty insulin syringe on the nightstand, so I know he's ready for breakfast. The jeans have a small hole by the zipper where his penis sits and I'm thinking if the hole wears any bigger his one-eyed mouse might poke out.

He sees me watching. "What's on the agenda for today, m' dear?"

I'm on my back and I stretch my arms above my head, raise my feet flat toward the ceiling. I have an idea I've been saving for him. "Mmm. Feel like some fun?"

He grabs me by the feet and pushes my legs onto the bed. Before I can move he's flopped part on top of me. He makes smooching noises into my neck with his mouth and I get chills and want him again. I grab his hand and put it on my tit. He stops nuzzling when he sees I'm breathing hard and rolls aside.

"Juliette, Juliette, what art thou?"

I climb over to straddle his stomach, touch the hole at his crotch with my pinkie. "Call me a nympho," I say, "but what's in a name?"

"*Nymphet* is more like it," he says. "Clever this morning."

"I saw the movie." I don't tell him how much I've thought about this, that he is my only Romeo, no matter how many times I hear it, the two of us against the world. I know it's a little too drippy sweet for him. In his view, we're Punch and Judy, puppets in a cruel universe. He says being black is like having the hump-back. Maybe so, but I'm not going to change my name to Judy.

I cup my fingers around his neck and grin. "Okay, first we go to Camille's for an Eggs Benedict Florentine – and then get a dog."

"A dog?"

"Yeah, from the pound – an old one – with personality – that likes cats. We don't have time to raise a puppy."

"Throw your clothes on," Punch says. He doesn't question my ideas and I don't question his. That's the deal. Besides, I keep him intrigued. He knows there's more, that I've got something to nudge his creativity for the book.

I fling a thin dress over my head and step into a thong and flip-flops, my tropic basics. They're the only kind of clothes I wear anymore.

As we walk down the row at the pound, I try not to look inside too many cages. I ask to see the oldest dog. The woman's not sure, but she takes us way back in the corner to a miniature Yorkie. He starts wagging.

She scoops him out. "He was rescued from an empty house. We think drug dealers and prostitutes left him there. He didn't have food, just a little saucer of beer."

"He's perfect," I say to Punch. "He'll think we're wonderful just for feeding him."

"Whatever you want, sweetheart – if you think we can keep up his beer habit. It's your gig."

"His name's Dollar Bill," the woman says. "You might want to change it."

I tell her it's fine. "Bill," I say. I give him a pet on the head.

She takes Bill and leads us to the front. We pay the fee and walk toward the door.

"Wait. I almost forgot," she calls to me. "Don't give him any stuffed bears."

"Huh? Why not?"

She walks closer staring at a piece of paper in her hand. "I don't know. That's what his card says."

"Must be those little plastic eyes," I say. "You know – they swallow them."

She nods.

We brought the car and Punch drives since it's before his noon happy hour, and I want to hold the dog. I stroke the bony little head.

"Okay," I say to Punch, "Since you're legally blind, we might as well get some advantage out of it – I mean you deserve to have a seeing eye dog, right?"

Punch frowns. "Yeah, sure."

"Well, I was thinking that we can take the dog to restaurants and clubs, wherever we want."

Punch gives me his weirded-out look, eyebrows thrust forward like shelves. "That's the reason we got him? This two-pound little shit for a fucking guide dog?"

"Not the only reason," I say. I hesitate, but I want Punch to get my meaning. "I'll have him for company when you're mad at me."

He laughs, something he doesn't do too often, and I'm glad I haven't spoiled the mood. "He's your type all right. Amazing genital proportions for such a small body."

I cluck my tongue because he always changes the subject. I don't want to harp on Punch's anger, so I drop it. Everybody has bad moods. I try not to take it personal. It's just the shit deal the world has always handed him. He's too sensitive and intelligent to float like me.

When we get home I set Bill on the floor and put down water and some Kal Kan we picked up. I pull out a catalogue I've been saving, where I first got this idea. It's for blind people. "Wonder how they read it," I say to Punch. My laugh comes out in a snort. I call up the 800 number and order the smallest guide dog halter they've got. Punch keeps chuckling the whole time I'm on the phone and I can barely say the catalogue number.

When I hang up Punch is at his computer so I stretch out on the tile next to Bill. He's panting, but his posture is relaxed, eyes bright.

"I want to try him in a restaurant first," I say.

"Okay, babycakes." I hear Punch's voice trail off, and I'm not sure he's heard what I said. I know he's already heavy into the writing and the Cuba libre next to him. Maybe he's adding our dog to his story. I can hardly wait till Bill's gear comes and we can take him out on the town.

3

◆◆◆◆◆◆◆◆◆◆◆◆◆◆◆◆◆

We get to Nina's, the Cajun place, around eight, prime time to catch the crowd of tourists. Nina's has nice atmosphere and fancy table settings with beads and fringe to give the feel of New Orleans. I usually try the weirdest item on any menu, but I'm already thinking fried mushroom salad and seafood gumbo, like I've had before.

We eat here a lot so we're in costume not to be recognized. I got most of the stuff at the thrift shop. Punch has a gray beard, dark sunglasses and his hair tucked inside a felt mobster hat. He's got his contacts in though. He figured it would be easier to play the role truly blind, but not any fun. I'm in a tight, black lycra number, spike heels, curly red wig, and pince-nez glasses I can look over. With the lipstick and pale powder I even fooled Punch. He looked up from his computer and did a double-take.

I'm thinking of myself as an entertainer. It's my duty to concoct cheap thrills for people that lack the energy or imagination to do it themselves. Of course, I'm hoping for some quirky humor for Punch's book. I don't interfere with his art, just set up interesting situations to stimulate it. I figure everything I put in motion has a chance to save our lives, but I can't tell Punch that.

We prance inside with Bill in the lead, tiny, but erect, and looking like a born guide. Punch has the leash in one hand and a dowel I painted white with a red tip in the other. I hold his left elbow. He bumps the door frame with his shoulder to get into the spirit. There's a crowd in line, but a path clears to let us in front. Besides being wacky, this routine might turn out practical. I feel a little funny taking advantage of people's good will, but it's only dinner.

Punch knocks a beer out of a big guy's hand. To me, it seems intentional. I'm thinking, shit. I should have known he'd take it too far. I give Punch a dirty look, which he has no problem remembering to pretend he doesn't see.

The guy's husky and hairy, like Grisly Adams, and his voice booms out, "No problem, man." He bends down to pick up the bottle that's spewing on the floor. Luckily it's still in one piece. Punch mumbles, "Sorry," and moves his cane forward. I see what's coming but can't do a thing, and when the guy straightens up, the cane separates his cheeks deeply and perfectly.

"Punch," I whine.

Punch pays no attention and leans farther. Grisly has to catch himself on a bar stool. He spins around. I can only hope Punch's face is innocent because this guy doesn't seem the type to go for a goose, even though we are in Key West.

Grisly stares a second with his eyebrows up and then turns to set his bottle on the bar.

"You motherfucker," I whisper to Punch. "You deserve whatever you get." Nothing's really funny, but trying to hold in a laugh makes me nearly explode. When Punch whispers back I can't hear him. Just the tickle of his voice in my ear is too much. I cover my mouth and run for the ladies' room. Punch can face the bear by himself. I hope nobody sees me cracking up. I don't want to blow our act on the very first night.

I pass a tall black-haired woman on my way back out to the

table. She's giving me a look, a wink and a smile. I don't know if she's flirting or onto our game.

I look across the room and see Grisly concentrating on his beer. He looks peaceful. Maybe he enjoyed it after all. Punch is seated at a table in the corner with Bill underneath. The waiter is reciting the menu, including prices. I look around to see if anybody is staring. Nobody is. Fuck no – it's Key West. I sit down and wait to order one of the sweet micro-brewery wheat beers, a big eighteen-ouncer, and feel how good it is to be with my man and my dog. We're doing just what we want, screwing with civilization a little, and not hurting anybody. I'm figuring that Grisly didn't react because the situation was too weird to figure. I guess if you quit trying to use reason you can get away with murder, even take your cute little dog to a restaurant.

I peek under the table at Bill. He's sitting up, taking everything in. "Look, Punch, Bill's all excited. I bet he likes Cajun food."

"I can't see, my dear, remember?"

Punch orders steamed crawfish, jambalaya and a double tequila. When the crawfish come I grab one and break off its head, suck out all the juices while I give Punch a sexy eye. I can't tell if he's looking behind those dark glasses.

I grab another one and break the meat out of the tail, feed it to Bill under the table, slurp at the head. "I can steal all your food," I whisper, "because you can't see a thing."

He whispers back. "I know you're sucking head, darlin'. My hearing is acute."

"You're a cute son-of-a-bitch all right."

He starts feeling across the table like he's trying to locate his tequila. I put my hand in his path and he fumbles as if surprised, then takes my fingers to his mouth.

"Ouch!" I pull my hand back and look at my knuckle where he nipped it.

"Sorry. Thought it was a crawdad." He chuckles and reaches for my hand again and kisses it.

"It didn't really hurt."

I start into my mushroom salad and watch him as he works by feel, eating and piling carcasses on an empty plate.

"What do you want to have in your stomach when they do the autopsy?" I ask. I like to bring up the subject. Maybe it'll make death seem less appealing to Punch in the long run. "I've been making a list."

He's chewing so I start first. "I want a sexy, exotic feast," I say, "a combination that'll make the autopsy memorable, stuff like I've seen on the Cooking Channel – fois gras with truffles, dim sum, gnocchi with pesto, chile rellenos, and for dessert, a spotted dick under a sugar cage decorated with edible flowers."

"A spotted dick, huh? That's easy to arrange."

"I could just eat myself to death and not even have to take the pills. What do you want in your stomach?"

"Wild Turkey."

"Oh, Punch. You have to eat. I want to have a nice meal together before the parade."

He grunts. "I'll eat some of yours."

"The fuck you will." I grab his last crawfish and guide it towards my open mouth to show him what it feels like. His face looks instantly resigned and I think he must've given up a lot of stuff in his life. I drop the crawfish back on his plate. "Shit," I say.

Punch finishes his tequila and holds the empty glass in the air for another. He's a natural blind man. "Where are you gonna get all that food anyway, Jul?"

"Can't I have fun thinking about it?" I say. "That's what we're in Key West for, isn't it? Fun."

"Yeah. It's a hell of a good time discussing our stomach contents when we're dead. Anyway, I told you, you've got no business following a feeble alcoholic to the grave."

"Oh, Punch."

He shakes his head. "Sweetheart, anybody ever tell you you're a strange chick"

"Always," I say. I brighten right up. "Strange" is always a compliment.

I reach under the table to pet Bill. Punch grabs my hand and pulls it to his crotch. I have to bend forward to reach where he's taking me. I gasp. "Umm," I say. He's unzipped and has half a hard-on sticking out under the table. I curl my fingers around it and give it some strokes. He's smiling with a vacant blind look.

I can't stay hunched in that position too long and I sit up straight. I lift my side of the tablecloth to see why Bill's so quiet.

"Bill's gone!" I yell. I jump up and look around. Punch remembers to stare unflinching while I scan the floor. It's not a big place and I'm thinking Bill ran outside or got back to the kitchen. Then I spot his leash coming under a corner table. He's with the woman who smiled at me. "There he is," I tell Punch.

I head over and reach down for the leash. She feeds him something. "I'm sorry," I say. "He's still in training."

She looks at me and starts laughing, tries to get out some words, but can't. She motions me to sit down and I do it.

I think I'm about to get a lecture, but I look at her twinkling eyes and giggle. We laugh until she takes a drink of her wine and blots her mouth on a napkin. She leans forward and whispers, "That man's not blind and that dog's too old to be trained."

"Please don't tell," I say. "We don't mean any harm."

She shakes her head. "Don't worry. I won't spoil your fun. You're entitled to it. Everybody is."

"Oh, it's not just for fun. Hard to explain."

"Whose idea was it, yours or his?" she asks.

I point to Bill and laugh. "His," I say. I don't know why it matters. "Mine really."

She nods, but doesn't look like she believes me.

"Really," I say.

She laughs and pushes a lock of gray hair off her face. There's just a little gray on the sides, like Punch. She has beautiful fine skin and her crystal earrings reflect the sparkle in her eyes. She seems somewhere in her thirties, extra self-assured. She puts a card in my hand. "Call me if you want to have lunch sometime. I know a place where dogs are encouraged."

Now I'm sure she's trying to pick me up. I look at the card. "Garden of Earthy Delights," it says, with a phone number and an address.

"It's my shop – books, crystals, herbal potions. I'm Isis."

"Juliette."

"I'm a lesbian, Juliette, but I see you like men."

I feel uncomfortable and look over at Punch. The waiter's handing him another tequila. I wonder if he's zipped his fly. "I better get back."

"Call me, if you get a chance – as a friend."

I stoop and put my finger in Bill's harness and back him out, smiling, but I'm wondering if she's implying something about me and Punch – that he's got my time all tied up or I need a friend. "Maybe I'll come by your shop," I say. "It sounds interesting."

On the way back to the table I'm figuring that Punch is on double tequila number three and maybe I missed one in there. I hope he can keep up his act on the way out.

I pass the waiter and ask him for another beer.

When I sit down Punch looks at me. "You wanna bring her home? I don't mind watching."

"Yeah, sure." I don't even look up. I don't want to acknowledge his drinking sense of humor. My gumbo's barely warm so I'm shoveling. It's good and I want to finish it before Punch decides we need to go. It's not that he means to cut me off, but after a few drinks he's in his own world. He never notices I'm still eating. Besides I don't want to risk hanging around until the whole evening goes to hell.

Punch orders another tequila. He sips and I manage to finish and pay the check without a problem. I hand him Bill's leash. At first he shakes his head, then takes it. I help him out of his chair because he really needs help.

"You're my angel," he says.

Sure enough his fly's still part open, but nothing's sticking out. If Punch was sober it would be funny, but by this point I just want to get him home to bed. I put my arm around his waist and guide him through the door.

I'm thinking if only Punch would've drank a little less, Bill's restaurant debut would be a funny incident and we could have fallen into bed together laughing, with Punch nuzzling my tits and pussy till we both totally lost control. But I know he can't stop. I don't know what he'd do without me to take care of him. As it is, I wonder whether Punch will even make it through the year, much less finish the book. I know he doesn't realize how bad off he gets or how I worry. At least I've got Bill to hold on my lap tonight, and that's something to put a little smile on my face.

4

◆◆◆◆◆◆◆◆◆◆◆◆◆◆◆◆◆◆

In the morning I wake up in the chair. I feel chilled. There's a smell of fried onions. It's the first time I never made it to bed. I'd been waiting for Punch to come in off the porch, but he must've passed me by. The last thing I remember is petting Bill. I look around, but don't see him. I wonder if Punch remembers any details from the restaurant to put into the book.

I walk into the kitchen and grab him from behind, squeeze him around the stomach and hug my cheek against his clean white t-shirt. He doesn't startle, just lays the spatula on the stove and turns around. He takes my hair in one of his big hands and tilts my head back for a kiss. I feel waves of heat rush up my arms. His lips are warm and moist, his tongue sharp-tasting from nibbling raw onion.

"Mmm," I say. I feel myself juicing up.

"I have an idea for today," he tells me. He's excited.

I stand waiting. I'm horny, but happy he's his fun self.

"Let's eat first – garlic, onion, zucchini, and pepper-jack omelette."

I get a fork and napkin and sit at the table. He sets a steaming omelette in front of me with the bottle of Tabasco alongside and goes back for his. I doctor my eggs and dig in, thinking how good he makes me feel. He knows how I love food. Sometimes I give him ideas from the Cooking Channel, but let him do all the work. It's his way to spoil me in the morning after I've had to take care of him at night.

He sits down. I can smell the Ivory on his fresh-showered body all the way across the table. I watch part of his tan biceps below the short sleeve as he lifts his fork.

He looks at me, swallows. "M' dear, m' dear, m' dear, m' dear," he says.

He takes another bite. I take another bite. I never ask what. He'll tell me when he's ready.

"I want to visit the Hemingway House."

"Again?" We've already been so many times I could give the tour, and I've gone there twice on my own he doesn't know about. We go through all the "m' dears" again. I laugh. Somebody else might get impatient and add a knuckle sandwich to his diet, but I know there's no meanness toward me. He thinks he's being cute – that I never get tired of him. It's basically true. I'm not really tired of the Hemingway House either.

"I need some inspiration," he says finally, "some atmosphere for the novel."

"Whenever you're ready," I say. Thinking about the book, I feel my energy and my hopes pick up. "I guess we'll have to leave Bill home." I've already scarfed the omelette and I go to the sink and splash my mouth.

"Tonight," he says.

"I think they close around seven."

"By ourselves, after dark, m' dear, m' dear, m' dear, m' dear."

I rinse my plate and reach for his. "Break-in?" I try to sound neutral, but I've never done anything like that.

"That's the important part – the excitement."

"I don't want to spend my last months locked up."

Punch gives me a look. According to our rules I'm not supposed to raise objections or ask for details.

"Whatever happens is experience," he says, "but we're not going to jail."

Nothing's good or bad, I remind myself, just interesting or boring. I trust his judgment, but sometimes the drinking messes things up. "Should be interesting," I say. I already feel curious, but I'm wondering if Punch can hold off the alcohol enough even to get started.

Sure enough. At midnight we dress in black sweatshirts and jeans and head out. We try to take the bikes, but Punch's has a flat because he hardly uses it. He needs to get some kind of exercise for his blood sugar, so we walk down Catherine to Whitehead, pass the front entrance of Hemingway House, turn right down the side wall on Olivia Street. I'm so excited, I feel like skipping. Punch is straighter than I've seen him at night in months and he's got his camera. He hands me a finger-sized flashlight he must have bought for the gig. We step out of the streetlights into the shadows of the wall and overhanging trees around the house, and I cover my hair with a black cap and take a briquet from my pocket to darken my face. Punch shakes his head like he can't believe how silly I look, but hell, it's another detail he can use for our story.

Punch tells me we have to be quiet because a security guard lives above the garage farther down the Olivia Street side. We round the corner to climb the five-foot brick wall under foliage. Punch gives me a boost and we drop onto vine-covered ground. Everything's soft and smells moist. A clump of seven or eight big cats watch us as we turn and slowly make our way toward the back. I follow Punch past a cat hospital area of small cages at the back of the house. We're on a sightseeing tour, it seems. We cross the patio near the famous Sloppy Joe urinal with the Spanish olive jar mounted above it. It's supposed to be the cats' watering trough, but it's dry. Punch turns to take a piss in it. I guess this is necessary. Probably always wanted to piss where Hemingway did. I try to pet a cat, to see the six toes – the Hemingway cat trait – but it backs up and runs. Punch finally shakes off and zips.

We round the building and I follow him up the steps to the front porch where we're standing next to tall shutters in spotlights that surround the house. I feel like I'm in a line-up already and look around wondering how we're supposed to get in, hoping he doesn't plan on breaking something. I always feel bad when things get broken. Anybody's things. It makes me cringe even in the movies.

I'm trying to remember if there are any alarms. Probably not much threat from literary worshippers to destroy old Hemingway stuff. It's not like Jim Morrison's grave.

Punch pulls his hand out of his jeans' pocket. I'm expecting to see a shiv or some gadget I really don't want to know he owns, but he has a key.

"Where'd you get that?" I whisper.

He smiles his that's-for-me-to-know look, and I relax a little, thinking one of his bar budds maybe set this up and we're not really breaking and entering.

Punch turns the knob and the door opens. I shut it quietly behind us. He turns right and I see the number pad for an alarm. I'm ready to panic, but he takes out a slip of paper and starts pressing buttons with his knuckle.

We screw in the heads of our flashlights and shine spots of light on the wood floor. Punch tugs my shirt to get me in motion and wanders into the living room–reception area on the right. It's stuffy and musty with the windows closed. I walk the perimeter and shine my light on the cat figurines and Hemingway books in fancy cabinets. I've seen it so many times I could walk around blindfolded, but I feel the thrill of touching what Papa Hems touched. It's exciting, being in the wrong place at the wrong time for no explainable reason. I bet Hemingway would get a laugh over it.

I walk to the rear where Punch is sitting on the antique love seat. He drops a white chain used to keep people from sitting down and runs his fingers over the wood trimmed edges like it's still an elegant piece. All the stuff looks nice in the dark. I wait while he lies back and puts his feet up. I'm getting antsy about how long we've been here and I glance over my shoulder out the window, but there's nothing, just trees and darkness. I figure Punch wouldn't be enjoying this so much if he couldn't make me nervous. He's testing me and I'm determined to pass.

He stands up and knocks the cushions to the floor, searching for change or relics, maybe crumbs, God knows. I heard some-body paid thousands for a crumble of Elvis's bacon inside a plastic marble. What would they pay for a Hemingway pube?

Punch gets down on his knees and sticks his face into a crack where an arm meets the base. I don't have a clue, but it won't help to ask. I stand there with my hands on my hips while he moves around the edge from one side of the couch to the other spreading the crack between the cushion and the base and putting his face into it. I think he might be having a sexual experience. Myself, I'm starting to sweat.

Finally he stands up and takes my hand. "I'm sucking in the creative molecules," he says. "You never know where inspiration comes from, where the muse is hiding."

I give him a weird look and he kisses my forehead. "Just kidding, babycakes."

I know he's serious and it makes me ache with love and the need to help him. He's so desperate to write this book – it's the one feeling he can't cover up.

I linger while he moves through the rear door and turns into the kitchen. I bend and suck a quick breath from between the sofa back and the armrest and dash into the kitchen.

Punch is at the sink that Pauline had elevated so Papa H.

could be comfortable cleaning his fish. No doubt she lived to regret it. The original height was probably his excuse to get out of chores – it hurt his back to bend or something, and she called him on it. I bet he never used it anyway, just napped after he stopped off at Sloppy Joe's, and it was damn uncomfortable for Pauline standing on tiptoe gutting those groupers and snapping beans or whatever. It's the price of living with a genius.

Punch reaches up and takes the plaque with the lobster shell off the wall, the one Hemingway mounted himself.

"Punch!" I whisper and grab his forearm.

He shushes me and moves sideways to break my hold.

Now I recognize this as burglary and I'm heading fast down the hall for the front door, figuring we got what we came for and it's time to dash. I hear Punch running after me and he gets his hand in the waist of my pants and stops me dead.

"Not yet," he says in my ear. I wait while he sets the lobster on the monk's bench and I'm hoping he'll forget about it and we'll be better off.

He nudges me toward the stairs. When we reach the top he takes a right into the master bedroom. I shine my light around and catch the midwife's chair in front of me alongside the bed. It's a foot-wide wood chair, without arms, so the poor woman couldn't fall asleep without landing on the floor. As if she could sleep with Pauline screaming in labor. I imagine she screamed – who wouldn't? That's something I'm glad to miss out on.

Punch is behind me and I feel my shirt being lifted over my head. I let him do it and turn for him to unzip my jeans. His fingers slide down my thighs. Finally the whole thing makes sense. I can dig sex in Hemingway's bed – anywhere really – I'm a Sagittarius. Punch read that Sagittarians would screw on a wet grave. I said, "Their mother's?" It was a joke.

I step out of my pants and sandals and wait for his mouth on mine and his hands on my tits. He kisses me, a nice one, and guides me towards the bed. He pulls back the heavy tapestry spread and there aren't any sheets, just an old striped mattress, but I hop in anyway. I lay back on the pillow and imagine Papa, his big paw pushing my head to the side while he kisses my neck. I look at Punch and open my legs.

"Pretend I'm Pauline," I say. "I just stole you away from Hadley."

Instead of taking off his clothes Punch backs up and lifts his camera.

"Hold the light on your face so I can see what I have," he says.

I do it.

"Fuck," he says. "You have that charcoal all over your cheeks."

"You never told me I needed to model."

"Go in there and wash it off." He motions me toward the bathroom, where the guides say Hemingway used to sit on the toilet and hold conversations with friends out on the front walk. I move a piece of wood frame that's blocking the doorway from tourists, cross to the sink in the corner, and do my best with the cold water faucet. I can barely see with the slight filtered light from the street. There's no soap. Time is passing. I slosh water around to clean up. I hope I haven't gotten black on the fancy decorative towel.

I get back in bed and Punch steps forward and places me in the famous Marilyn pose, on my side with my elbow out by my head, except he fixes my legs so my pussy shows. It's his deal, so I do my best with a sexy smile. I pouf up my hair to look more glamorous.

"I'm going to try different effects. I have some filters for the flash."

"What if somebody sees light in the window?"

"Not likely. Plenty of trees around."

I'm not so sure, but I act cool and give him a pouty look. He's making soft "mmm's" like he's ready to eat me. He never gets enough of looking at me when he's sober. It'll be fun to have these pictures of our craziness to look back on. I bet it'll make good details for the book. Maybe for publicity later.

Punch is changing film when we hear a door open downstairs. I suck in air.

"Sssh," Punch says low.

We hear footsteps in the hall. The person isn't trying to sneak.

Punch bends over me. "Just keep quiet," he whispers. "He probably won't come up."

The next footstep is on the stairs, a hollow creak, a steady pace. I'm frozen. I know he'll head right to this room because the door's open and it wasn't before. I'm feeling unusually naked. There's no way out. Punch steps behind the door. Like an idiot I yank the heavy cover over my head and flatten out. I'm thinking I should have gotten under the bed, but it's too late. The footsteps pause at the door. I see the glow of a flashlight through the heavy weave of the bedspread. I wait for the sound of a cocking gun, like in the movies.

There's a sharp thwack. Then a heavy thud. A bump. The cover is whipped off me.

Punch stands looking down. "Get your wee ass moving," he yells.

I make out a guy on the floor next to the midwife's chair that's knocked over.

I gasp. "Is he dead?"

Punch has me by the arm. He's pulling me off the bed, but my feet are tangled in the spread.

"Fuck, no! He's fine. Let's get out of here!"

He picks me up and the spread falls off. He sets me on my feet and I bend to look for my clothes. They're kicked under the bed or somewhere.

"No time," he says.

I look at him. I don't see how I can run all the way home naked. I grab the spread. Punch pushes me toward the door and

I hold the thick cover balled up as we run down the stairs. Punch turns back to scoop up the lobster plaque and stick it under his shirt. We dash out to the gate but there's a lock on the inside.

Cats follow close behind us as we make our way around the wall. Punch runs toward a birdbath. I follow close. He puts his foot in the direct center so it won't tip, gets on the wall, and reaches a hand down for me. I'm still holding the spread, but I put my foot into the slimy bowl and grab his ankle. I get my other knee on top of the wall and pull up beside him. The stone is wet and rough and I feel my ass cheeks and legs scrape as I push myself over and jump to the sidewalk. I hold the spread in front of me and we run close to the wall under the trees, moving fast all the way to Catherine Street. I'm out of breath with the heavy spread and all the excitement. My feet are bruised and stinging.

Punch turns into the street, which is really more like an alley and pulls me behind a bouganvillea thick with blooms. He's breathing harder than I am. He points. "Somebody might recognize that blanket. You'd better leave it here. You can have my shirt."

The T-shirt is long enough for a dress so I'm well covered and not noticeable. Punch is sweaty and his chest shines like new brass in the moonlight. I look at him and feel great. We got away without being seen. I start to laugh.

Punch looks at me and laughs too. I'm ecstatic. I grab his arms and we keep laughing, falling into each other, him trying to muffle it into my shoulder, me into his chest. It's a hell of an adventure.

"So that's why you're called Punch!" I shriek. We can't stop laughing. I snort and laugh more. I know we shouldn't make so much noise, but I'm high with nerves and relief.

A car heads our way. We quiet down, our stomachs jerking from cooped up laughs. Punch pulls my head back and kisses me, and I solder myself to his mouth, knowing he's the only man I'll ever want, no matter what happens, no matter if I had a hundred more years to look around.

The car passes and he takes my hand to start walking. He's got his lobster and I look at Papa's bedspread on the ground. Some bum will wrap himself up in it to sleep and that's probably a good use, but I don't want to leave it.

"Hang on," I say to Punch. I shake out some of the leaves and fold the spread in thirds. I lift the shirt, wrap the spread around my body, tuck it in across my tits, and smooth the T-shirt down. I look like I'm wearing an ankle-length fringed skirt underneath.

Punch nods. "Not bad. You're even gorgeous in a bedspread."

We walk the rest of the way home and the few people we pass pay no attention to my get-up.

When we get there Punch heads for the rum and I pick up Bill. He's all licky and waggy, like we've been gone for a week. I pull off my bedspread and arrange it like a nest on the couch and try to coax Bill onto it. He's not interested, but Punch comes over with his drink. He offers me a swig. Instead I put my mouth on his. It's sweet with orange-pineapple juice and rum, a kick for his blood sugar. I get my tongue into the space between his lips and teeth and suck his tangy potent flavor into me.

He picks me up against his bare chest and takes me to bed. I feel heat flow over me. He's not usually sober enough at night to want me. He lays me gently on the bed and I see the softness come into his eyes when he goes down on me. I can see the love there, how much care he's taking. I'm sweating down the backs of my thighs and flowing my juice down his chin while we lick and suck each other. He gets his cock half hard and rolls to the side, picks me up like I'm light as air and sets me on his hips. I glide his cock into me, keeping it inside with my fingers, squeezing hard inside till I come. I drop on his chest drained.

I wake up when Punch goes for a refill on his drink. He comes back from the kitchen and slides next to me.

"I didn't know you could knock a guy out so easy," I say.

He pauses. "Not that easy. I know how to throw a punch, but it was mostly luck."

"He'll be okay, won't he?" I'm trying to sort the reality from what happens in the movies. I think of the pain. My stomach gets queasy.

"Don't worry. Men are used to taking a hit here and there. You grow up with it. No big deal."

I turn on my stomach to make it feel better and put my cheek against his shoulder. "Will they be looking for us?"

"It's no big deal. Anyhow, I had to play it out by then."

I'm thinking, number one, we didn't have to go there, and number two, we could've maybe talked to the guy. At the same time I'm mad at myself for not being able to control my feelings. I need to do that if I'm going to keep my resolutions for a wild life and stick by Punch. I know nothing matters in the end for anybody. I rejected the idea of justice and the hereafter long ago. I was never a good Presbyterian girl.

"Where'd you get the key and alarm code?" I ask.

"Guy I know at Tony's. I'll give the key back tomorrow."

"I just hope the guard's all right." My feelings slide lower from there, because I start thinking about tomorrow night when I know Punch will drag home from Tony's barely conscious on his rum. I wonder if he'll live through the abuse of his body even the five months we have left.

5

◆◆◆◆◆◆◆◆◆◆◆◆◆◆◆◆

The next morning Punch says we should listen to the news to see if there's any mention of our escapade. The way he's moving around shows he's nervous, like I am. I sit on the couch with Bill in my lap when it's time for the noon update from Miami. Sure enough, they mention us – "Stay tuned for details on the bizarre robbery at the Hemingway House in Key West."

I look at Punch and he gives me an eyebrows-up. He sits down and puts his arm around me.

"I wish I would have taken my clothes," I say.

We wait for fifteen minutes before they get to us. The anchorman is live, walking through the Hemingway grounds, pointing out the details. I'm amazed at how well he's got us pegged – where we climbed the wall both times and that we're male and female. "Presumably, the man stopped to relieve himself at the antique urinal," the reporter says. He's chuckling. "The woman left all her clothes upstairs in the master bedroom."

I cluck my tongue at Punch and we both laugh. I smack him on the thigh. "I should have peed too. Just to add volume." I'm giggling and feeling better because they're having fun with the story, not like it's a serious crime.

The newsman goes on to say that two valuable antiques have been taken. I'm looking into the kitchen at the lobster that Punch has hung above the sink. Bill is curled on the bedspread. "The estimated value of these items could be as much as $30,000 if sold to collectors. This is thought to be the motive for the crime."

My mouth drops open. I look at Punch and he's staring at the screen with his lips tight.

"Did you know that?" I ask him. "Punch?"

"No. No way," he says.

"On the serious side," the reporter continues, "a custodian, seventy-one-year-old Lawrence Hill, was seriously injured when a blow to the jaw knocked him down, causing his head to strike a chair. He's in intensive care, at Key West Community Hospital, and has not yet regained consciousness. Police are now in the process of collecting fingerprints and other evidence from the crime scene."

"Oh, God," I say. The news about the guard knocks all the air out of me.

"I didn't know he was so old," Punch says.

"Could he die?"

"No. Not from that little tap. It's a freak thing he's unconscious."

Now I'm really worried, about the guard and about us. "Fingerprints?" I say to Punch.

"A thousand people go through there each week. They can't possibly sort them all out."

I'm thinking of when I washed my face at the sink. Nobody on the tour is allowed in the bathroom.

"You've never been fingerprinted, have you?"

"No," I say. "What about you, Punch?"

"Once, but I was a juvenile. Those records were all destroyed."

I look at him and shake my head.

"Don't sweat it. Everything's fine. Worse case scenario, if they arrest us we can make bail, get a lawyer to keep our trial from coming up until it's too late."

"That doesn't make me feel any better."

He picks Bill off my lap and sets him on the floor. He takes my face in his hands and smooths my hair back. "You know I'll take care of you no matter what happens. It's you and me – together always."

"Worse case is if old Mr Hill dies," I say. I feel tears coming. I don't know how I'll stand it and I'm not sure how Punch can protect me. Then I stop thinking. Punch's hands on my face make me warm. I'm a sucker. All he needs to do is hold me. "What are we going to do with the stuff?"

"Keep it. They can take it back when we're gone."

"You're always ahead of me," I say. "That's what I like about you." I grab his face and kiss him.

"I don't think they'll connect Monty Rey – the guy who gave me the key. He had it made a couple years ago when he did some work there. He'd keep quiet anyway."

That night when Punch goes to Tony's I want to sit and watch the Food Channel, but I feel upset. They're doing mushroom quesadillas, and I start thinking about Viva Zapata. I can taste those margaritas and some nachos. I have to do something or lose my mind. I throw on a sundress and head out. I park the bike in the rack at Catherine and Duval to walk the short piece. A woman brakes beside me.

"Hey there," she says.

In a second I place her from Nina's. It's Isis.

I smile.

"We meet again," she says. She wants to know where I'm headed and I tell her. She asks if I mind company.

"If I did, I wouldn't be going to Viva's," I say. "It's really loud and somebody always starts talking to you."

"Sounds good to me. I haven't been there."

I'm wondering which bars are the lesbian ones where she might go. I know of one on Simonton.

We both order margaritas and I ask her if she wants to split nachos. She seems more than happy and I wonder if I should say it's just nachos I'm offering, no other kind of splits.

The music is much lower than usual. We sip our margaritas and she tells me about her shop. Jewelry, candles, incense, herbs, and potions are the main items.

"What kind of potions?" I ask.

"For spells."

"Witchcraft?"

"Yes. I sell ingredients and instructions for good spells. I'm a Wiccan, a white witch. It's my religion – worship of the goddesses of nature."

"Cool."

She nods.

I've heard of these spells, but never talked directly to a witch before. "I haven't noticed your shop."

"I keep it toned down. People find me when they need me. I'm not out to make a lot of money, just to live comfortably and offer my skills. I sold my shop in Salem a couple months ago, so I'm just getting started here."

"Wow," I say. "A witch from Salem. Sounds pretty authentic."

The nachos come and she picks up a chip with cheese, jalapenos, and guacamole. I'm watching her, thinking I wouldn't have expected a witch to eat nachos.

She chews and swallows. "I had a big following up there, but it was time to leave."

I have my mouth full so I don't have to ask why. From the sound of it she might mean something bad and I've had enough of that for one day.

She asks if I'm married to Punch.

The question makes me twitch. I realize there's not much chance I'll ever do that. "No," I say. "We've been living together for almost a year though. We dated for a year before that, then broke up for a while." I'm not comfortable enough to go into his diabetes and drinking and the year's plan.

She looks at me like somehow she knows all about us and thinks I'm making a big mistake. Maybe to her all men are bad for women – or she thinks she would be better for me.

"Do you live with somebody?" I ask her, hoping she does.

"No. I did in Salem, but she left me."

I'm awkward enough with the lesbian stuff and not ready for a sad story to boot. I wonder why the music isn't cranked up. I can't think of anything to say. We eat for a while.

"I need to get going," Isis says. "You should drop in to see me. I have potions you might be interested in. Something for your boyfriend."

"Hmm," I say.

"You have my card?"

"Yeah. Sure. It's in my purse."

She pecks me on the cheek, which I'm not expecting, and lays a ten on the bar. I watch her make her way through a grungy pack of guys outside the open entranceway. She's graceful and self-assured. I wonder if it's because she doesn't care a rat's ass about the men or if it comes from being a witch. I think I will go see her sometime. Now that I thought it, I'll have to do it.

I hang in for my other two margaritas, working my way through the rest of the nachos. "It's a real quiet night," I say to a young guy next to me, "like the opposite of a full moon or something."

He grunts. He's half in a trance. I look at my plate and clean up some cheese and sour cream with the last two chips.

I think about doing my flash routine again on the way home. I'm determined to make a workable scene out of that. Then I remember I need to buy a gun.

I get home before Punch, throw off my dress and take a

healthy pee. I spread out on the bed. I can pretend to stay asleep and not get in any arguments, but I have hours of worry till then and missing him next to me.

6

◆◆◆◆◆◆◆◆◆◆◆◆◆◆◆◆

It's May 1st, and Punch announces at breakfast that he's running a little behind on the book. He has a hundred pages on his proposed three-hundred, and with rewrites and all, he'll never get finished by Fantasy Fest at the end of October. We've been lounging around the nude pool at Atlantic Shores Motel for a couple hours' lunchbreak everyday – enjoying the scenery, bodies and ocean – but he's decided he needs to cut that to catch up. The book is the most important thing, but I'm thinking that this isn't the wild kind of living we planned, and if he could spend less time drinking and crashing, we could do it all.

I already spend enough time in the evening drooling in front of the Food Channel or hanging out on Mallory Dock at sunset, adoring the trained housecats. I used to like to watch the tourists loosen up in all the craziness. I'd stroll around like I'm one of the bohemian types they'd like to be. Sometimes I dance a little by myself for the street musicians, but it's tame without Punch, and we don't have much time left, if things stay like they are.

Punch repeats his plan to write all day, and I grunt in discontent. Then the thought hits me to go on to the pool myself and have my three fucking bloody Marys. I can read and sleep and swim all afternoon, and in practical thinking, we probably wouldn't have done anything wild anyway or even had much conversation. "Okay, I'll leave you in peace," I tell him. I throw on a sundress, touch the back of his neck with a kiss, and head out.

I lock up my bike at the rack in front of the pool and walk up the stairs to the deck. I pay my two bucks and follow the chair man between the chicki bar and the pool, across the concrete. I have him set me up with a lounge chair on the long wooden pier on the ocean. I don't feel like talking to any men, and there's nobody out there. I pull off my dress and thong, spread my towel, and stretch out in the breeze, looking up into a wispy cloud shaped like a kitten with a chopped-off tail.

The favorite trick is for a straight guy to pull a chair directly in front of me and turn on his stomach to look up my pussy. I'm usually amused by how cool they think they are and spread my legs wide enough so they have all they can handle. I get wet imagining their wankers squeezing out between those plastic strips, but I've never really been able to see under there. Punch gets a kick out of sitting next to me watching. He accepts my exhibitionism because he knows I'm true to him. He says there's no harm – I think he enjoys other guys getting silly over me – knows I like it. But he says if his old donkey popped through, he'd scrape himself raw on the concrete. Or if he's on a lounge in front of me, he says, "Good thing I'm used to looking at you or I'd have a bushel of splinters in my prick."

I don't say anything, but I'm thinking I wouldn't mind if he had that kind of problem. Not that his dick isn't big enough. He could almost fit that tattoo – "See you in Jamaica," or however the joke goes. But it's not often enough the sucker stiffens up. Once I told him about the pills to make it work better – easy, I saw it on TV. But he said he didn't want to mess with nature, and I get enough sex for any normal human being – he's not around to be my playtoy. "Why not?" I asked him. He didn't answer.

I wrap my towel around me to be polite, go to the bar, and order two bloody Marys. I take the plastic cups out to my chair. I like to drink the first two fast, then sip on the last one. After a nap and a swim I can have another session without getting plowed.

I wake up and the air is cool. Rumbling black and blue clouds have rolled across the sun. I feel the energy. A thunderstorm always whips up my spirits.

I throw on my sundress and panties and pick up my towel. The thin dress blows up and covers my head. I smooth it down and the wind flattens it against my body as I hurry back up the pier. I walk toward the covered bar area and it starts to pour. I know I'll never be able to ride my bike in that. I step up to the bar and order another bloody Mary.

"Hey there."

I turn left. It's Isis. She's wearing a brimmed hat, dangling earrings, and a wrap-around cover-up. The gray is covered by the hat and she looks much younger than before, black eyes sparkling. She sort of resembles a picture I have of my mother before she ran off to California.

She points to the chair next to her.

I look at the rain dancing in the pool. Lightning branches out across the horizon. I sit.

"It's my day off," Isis says, "a witch's holiday."

I'm not sure if she's teasing. "Not a good day to catch a tan." I'm noticing how white she is. Must be her first time here.

"It's nice though, isn't it? Thunderstorms are so energizing."

"Yeah," I say. "I was just thinking that."

I slurp my drink to the bottom of the cup. It's still raining hard. I pull out the lime piece and suck on it.

"I have my car," Isis says. "Why don't you come with me to see the shop. You would find it interesting."

It crosses my mind that this could be a new area for discovery. Maybe something Punch can use in the book.

We head north on Duval and take a right at Angela Street. Isis parks three doors down in front of a two-story white clapboard with a little gingerbread decoration around the eaves and the porch rail. There's a sign painted with flowers and leaves saying "The Garden of Earthy Delights." She leads me up the three steps. We pass a black cat sound asleep in a ball. The tail is short like a rabbit's. "What happened to its tail?" I ask.

"Oh, she's a manx – they're tail-less. Rather, her mother was a manx and her father a Persian, so she inherited a stub."

"She's beautiful," I say. I'm thinking – okay, a witch and her black cat. It's a must.

Isis nods and opens the door. "I just hired a young woman to work part-time. This is her first day alone."

Chimes tinkle and I smell incense with a tinge of something peppery. It's cool and quiet. Low mood music floats through light curtains at the back. Glassed-in cases of jars and bottles, and tables and shelves of candles, books, jewelry, chimes, crystals and packages of herbs fill up the room. It's all clean and new. A mural spreads across the back arch above the hall – three women's faces growing out of each other, all striking. The first is very young, then middle-age, then ancient. I think it's Isis in the middle.

A young girl, maybe seventeen, walks out from the back, she flows really, in a silky caftan. She's slim and pretty, with thick dark hair.

"Lily, this is Juliette."

"Welcome to the garden," she says. She puts out a delicate hand and takes mine. She seems serene. I never thought of that word to describe a young person before.

Isis asks her how the morning went, and I turn to look at what's on the table next to me. There are lots of fancy carved sticks that I take to be wands. I'm afraid to touch them. I pick up a plastic bag marked "Wolf Hair." I squeeze it. Sure seems to be the real thing.

"It's for spells, protection mainly – hair shed from a live wolf. I'll show you how to use it sometime."

I don't believe in this stuff, but sure, it starts me thinking that it couldn't hurt.

Isis invites me in back for a cup of chamomile tea. I can hear rain on the metal roof all the way from upstairs. I follow her. I'm thinking I should bring Punch here to look around.

The back room is her kitchen and the rest of her living space is upstairs. She fixes the tea in a fancy teapot, measuring tea leaves, and setting everything just so, on a silver tray. I haven't had real tea since I was a little girl. Tea and toast for the mumps or whatever. Grammy would come over when I had to stay home from school and Pop had to work at the church.

I'm getting an old-fashioned, homey feeling with the fragrant tea and the storm outside. I feel calm for a change. We sit across from each other at the table and I tell Isis about Punch and how we're living here for a year while he writes his novel. I mention his drinking and diabetes, but I don't dare say the final step in our plan.

She suggests that there are herbs and potions to help with that, but I tell her I don't know. The idea gets my hopes up, but I'm thinking the stuff is probably real expensive, and Punch would never do it.

She doesn't push it. We talk about Key West till the rain stops. "I'll give you a ride to your bike," she says.

I take my empty cup to the sink where she's set the tray. She turns to me and puts a hand to my hair. She strokes it back behind my ear, letting her cool fingers trail down my neck and across my bare shoulder. It could be a come-on, but it's so tender and motherly, I stay still. I'm not afraid of her – I'm curious.

She looks into my eyes and her other hand caresses my

chin. She tilts my head forward and kisses my forehead. I don't mind.

The rain has stopped and I tell her I'd like to walk home since it's all fresh outside. She smiles and walks me to the door.

"Thanks for the tea," I tell her.

"Anytime you like."

I'm not in a hurry. On my way, I see a white stuffed bear in a store window. It reminds me of Bill. I'm thinking that if somebody bothered to say don't give him a stuffed bear, maybe I should. Punch says when people warn you against something, it's usually pretty good – at least worth a shot. I can't resist buying it. I figure I'll keep an eye on him, in case those plastic eyes are a problem.

I get home around three and Punch is asleep on his back on the couch. I pet Bill and set the bag with the bear on the end table. The screen-saver is up on the computer and a watery drink sits beside the keyboard. I wonder what number drink it is – and how many pages Punch has written – but I'd never look at his writing without him knowing. I saw *The Shining* – I'm no fool!

I walk over to the couch, bend down and kiss his cheek lightly. He feels cold to my lips, damp. He looks paler than I've ever seen him. He should be hot and sweaty in this room, not clammy. I touch his forehead with my hand. The coolness scares me.

"Punch, Punch," I shake his shoulder. I cradle his head in my hand and rub his cheek. He doesn't move. His head is heavy, his neck wobbly like a baby's.

I start to think clearer and put my hand on his throat for a pulse. It's there. I think. I put my ear near his mouth. I can feel breath. I think.

I slap him. Slap him again harder on the other side. Slap him again harder, again, again. I see some pink come into his cheeks. I'm not sure that it means anything. "Punch," I keep yelling. "Punch, wake up."

His eyes open to slits. I feel some movement of muscle in his neck, but he's not looking at me, just staring across the room. "Punch, are you okay?"

He struggles to sit up. I help prop him, lean him back against the couch. His skin is a gray-white, except where I slapped him. I don't know whether his blood sugar is high or low. All I know is to try orange juice. I ask if he wants some, but he doesn't answer. I go for it.

I hand him the juice and he drinks the six ounce can down.

"Thanks," he says. He shifts on the couch. "Now get me a rum and coke, so I can pep up. I didn't mean to take a nap this afternoon."

I look at him. Sweat glistens on his forehead.

"Please, Jul, get me a rum and coke."

"You weren't napping. You were passed out."

"So you've been using me for a punching bag, while I'm sleeping? What was it, an upper cut?"

"Not funny, Punch."

"No, and it's not fair either. *Punch* isn't short for punching bag."

I argue with him about seeing the doctor, but he insists he was just sleeping. He seems so sure of it, I wonder if I imagined a problem. I want to think so, forget his icy skin in an eighty-five degree room. I give up and go for the rum and diet coke. I feel like I'm feeding him poison, but that's the deal. He goes back to the computer.

I hear a rustle and look over to see Bill on the table yanking the stuffed bear out of the bag. It plops on the floor and he gives it a sniff. His ears go up and his posture changes. In three seconds he's mounted it. His tiny butt is pumping and his wet pink arrow of a penis grazes the bear's stomach.

"Punch, look!"

Five seconds more and Bill comes. A clear spurt of gissum glistens on the white fur.

"Believe that?"

"He's a horny critter," Punch says. "I told you he was your type."

"They probably trained him to do that," I say. I massage Bill's neck and behind his tiny ears. He ignores me and walks to the door. I put the bear up and take him outside.

Punch calls through the screen, "Hey, babycakes, let's eat at Gato Gordo tonight. Bill hasn't tried it yet. Just give me a couple more hours to work."

He knows how to cheer me up. I smile and throw him a kiss.

Bill snuffs around the plant beds, probably trying to find some unburied cat turds, a doggie gourmet treat. I take him over to the patio and tie him to a lounge chair. The sun is broiling. I strip off my dress. I've got plenty of time before I start putting on my costume for the restaurant. The water is cool as I trudge down the stairs. I keep going till my head is under. No sense worrying about Punch. I have to remind myself to live day by day.

7

◆◆◆◆◆◆◆◆◆◆◆◆◆◆◆◆◆

I wake up. Punch is leaning on his elbow staring at me. It's morning. "It's summer," he says. "I have a great idea."

It's my turn for an idea, but we never really made a rule about that. "Just so we don't have to break in anywhere," I say. I'm still nervous about the fingerprints. We haven't heard anything about the guard. I asked Punch to find out from his friends at Tony's, but he says nobody knows. Key West is a small-town island, so that's hard to believe, but I won't bug him.

I stretch and yawn. "Okay, it's June 1st, but it's been summer here forever."

Punch folds the flesh on his stomach and I watch him angle the tiny needle into his skin and plunge the insulin into his body. Such a small amount of liquid to keep him alive – a delicate thing to contend with the quarts of alcohol.

"We have a lot to do," he says. "I bought a motorcycle and we need to – "

"A motorcycle? When?"

"A used one. A Triton, Triumph Bonneville, 650 cc engine in a Norton Featherbed frame, like I've always wanted. I almost got one when I stayed in Liverpool."

It sounds real fancy to me. "How much?"

"I haven't paid for it yet. I have to pay today when I pick it up."

I'm trying to keep my eyeballs in my head and my mouth shut. Our money's going fast. I don't want to ask the price again.

"Is there a problem with that?" asks Punch.

We never made a rule about purchases. Our living expenses were set. "I don't think we have enough money, Punch," I say.

"That's interesting," he says. "I didn't tell you the price."

"We're pretty close on our budget," I say. I feel my defenses go up, because *interesting* doesn't mean just that. It's what he says to imply he's just found out something bad about me. And then he'll never say what it is, so I can't prove him wrong. I have to ask anyway. "What's interesting? Us not having enough money to buy a fancy, status symbol motorcycle?"

"It's a collector's item, an unbelievable deal, mint. This guy's desperate. We can make money – " He gets ticked off and stops talking, but since it's still morning and he hasn't had a drink yet, he goes into the bathroom and shuts the door instead of grabbing my shoulders and telling me I'm a phoney, and my white, middle-class standards are fucked, and I don't have a clue how the world works. Silence says it loud and clear.

I'm angry and I pause a second but then go to the door and start yelling through it. "How are you going to buy a bike unless it's with my fucking money?"

Now I know I've lost my head because this is something I promised I'd never say. Punch made me set up my own account and told me before we started that he wouldn't feel right living off money that was three-quarters mine. I told him it was Pop's until he died and now it's ours. Pop deserved to give it to Punch to pay back for all the meanness. It was never mine. I convinced Punch I wouldn't live to spend it without him. Now I've contradicted all that.

He doesn't answer and I can feel him thinking – that's

interesting, that's very interesting. It means down deep I'm holding his spending against him, and probably every drink, and he'll never be able to trust me again. I want to say that I didn't mean it, but with Punch you can't take anything back, no second chances. I start to feel sick at my stomach, thinking that this is the end of our life together. I'll go insane or die without him. But if I don't go insane or die, that's even worse.

I gag and run into the kitchen and the gagging turns into heaves. The sink is my only choice. My throat clenches and my stomach feels like it's rising with the sharp pain, but there's nothing but water inside of me. I run the tap to drown everything out. I don't know if Punch can hear me from the bathroom. In a way I wish he could – to know how much I love him and need him. Finally my stomach settles down. I dry my mouth on a paper towel and float lightheaded into the bedroom. I mash my face into the pillow, hoping he'll come to talk, but knowing he never has before. I sob and sob.

I wake up sweaty and check the clock. I've slept almost to noon. I get up and look for Punch. He's not inside. The computer's off and Bill's sleeping on the couch. I hope Punch has gone to get the bike, despite what I said, and he'll come home all happy with his new toy. Fuck the money.

It crosses my mind that I've been meaning to get a gun. It's a good time to do it. Punch likes guns – he likes a lot of the same things Hemingway did. I drag myself up and take a shower.

I ride my bike to Uncle Sam's pawn shop on Duval. The glass door is blacked-out, uninviting, but I open it and step inside. The guy behind the counter is maybe in his thirties, wearing a muscle shirt, not the nice older man I'd seen before. This guy's got dark hair in a ponytail and homemade tattoos, crosses on his forearms and women's names on both biceps. He reminds me of my mother's lover, the picture I kept of him from the paper after his arrest.

He doesn't say anything or move, just stares as I turn to look at the stuff. I'm uncomfortable, but I walk slowly down the glass case that takes up the whole right side of the narrow shop. The place is cool and dim yellow in florescent light except for dusty rays coming through the windows in front. There's a batch of typewriters and guitars, some watches and jewelry. I finally come to the guns and knives all the way in back, right in front of the guy and the cash register. I don't know anything to ask for and I wish I had on my restaurant disguise in case I sound stupid.

He doesn't move an eyelash. "I want to buy a gun," I say, "see some guns."

"Who ya plannin on shootin?" he asks.

I want to sound tough, so I tell him "Anybody that looks at me cross-eyed."

His eyebrows go up. He's digging it – like I'm the type could really shoot somebody.

He slides open the doors of the case he's leaning on, bends down and points to four handguns. "This is all I have right now." He points to the smallest one. "I'd recommend this .25 Beretta for a lady. Fits in your purse. Easy to handle for protection."

I guess I look like I need protection. It makes me think of Isis and the wolf hair. Maybe I'd be better off buying a packet of fur.

He sets a small black pistol and a much larger shining steel gun delicately on the glass in front of me, pointed his way.

"Go ahead and pick one up. You wanna get the feel in your hand."

I go for the little black one, put my finger in the trigger and curl my hand around the grip. It's smaller than a pocket camera, shiny black metal and plastic, compact and cool in my hand, like a quality-made toy. It seems like a nice fit, concentrated weight and power the size for my hand.

"That's a Beretta."

He puts grimy fingers on my wrist and manipulates the gun in my hand, showing me the pop-up barrel. "You load one round here and you can squeeze off eight shots as fast as you can pull the trigger."

He pushes the button so the empty clip slides out, room enough for seven tiny bullets. He cocks the hammer and moves my hand so I'm pointing toward the wall. He squeezes my finger on the trigger. It clicks. A chill of pleasure moves down my neck. I remember the first time I met Punch, with the gun under his jacket.

"Easy, huh?" he says. "The shells eject and you keep on going. You'd have to do that if you needed to kill somebody – unless you hit a major organ. One shot isn't going to take anybody out. It's not that powerful."

He picks it up like a toy in his big hand. He shows me the safety switch and a halfway position for the hammer that keeps the trigger from moving. He puts it back on the counter.

I pick up the big one. It's a monster.

"That's a Colt .45. The gunmetal has been coated to make it shiny, and ivory grips added. You could put somebody down or make 'em bleed to death with one shot easy."

"It's pretty," I say.

He puts his hand back over mine to support the weight. I feel his hot breath in my ear. I jerk my head back. I don't want anything to do with him.

I twist my hand to free it and clunk the gun on the glass counter.

He picks it up and pops open the top. "Here's the slide where you chamber a round." He snaps it shut, then cocks the gun and jams his palm against the front of the barrel. The slide moves back. "Look." He shows me his finger squeezing the trigger. No click. "Somebody with guts – who's close enough – can stop this gun from firing." He shows me again. "It's called a palm jam in the military – push hard and the slide goes back and locks. The gun won't fire. By the time it takes to release it, too late."

"That's interesting," I say. I stroke the bright metal. "But this is too heavy."

I point back to the first one. "How much is the little black one?" I ask.

He picks it up and aims toward the door. "Gunmetal blue, that is, Beretta .25 mm., never been fired – I can let it go for one-thirty."

"I wasn't thinking that high."

He frowns. "That's a good price. I don't have any junk. It's not worth the paperwork hassle to sell it for less."

I like the Beretta, for the handy size, and it's cute. I wonder if I should get Punch to look at it. I remember I'm trying to impress him. "Okay," I say. I pick up the gun and hand it over.

He gives me a form to fill out. "I need a $50 deposit. It's a three-day waiting period, but sometimes it takes a couple days longer."

"Oh?" I'd hoped to bring it home to Punch.

"Call before you come to pick it up."

I'm afraid Punch might think I'm spending too much, but fucking shit, he's either left me and I can shoot myself, or we're still tight and he's already spent thousands on a motorcycle.

I ride home and lock my bike outside the gate at the compound. Our Toyota is there, but I don't see any cycle. I take a breath, one heavy with sweet humidity and flowering boxwood. Mmm. It makes me feel a little better. I walk fast under the trees and out to the bright sunlight of the patio. Punch is on a chaise lounge, holding a plastic cup, talking to our neighbor Albin, who's a writer. Albin and I sun in our g-strings sometimes and talk about writers and his adventures, but this is the first time I've seen Punch have a conversation. I wonder why he isn't inside writing. I remember that Albin wrote obituaries for a lot of famous people before he retired – maybe Punch is trying to set something up for himself.

I say hi to Albin and walk past them and down the walk to

our cottage. Punch is still talking when I look back from the porch. I go in and get a Bud out of the fridge and sit down on the couch. My stomach feels syrupy, but the beer helps. When I'm halfway done, I start thinking I've had it with Punch. How can he stay out there knowing I feel like I could die and our whole life together is shot to shit. My stomach starts jumping again and my face is hot from tears I won't let come. He's the one supposed to be so desperate anyway.

Finally his feet scuff on the concrete steps. I straighten up and take a swig of beer.

His shadow falls onto the wood floor. He opens the screendoor. "Hey, babycakes."

My shoulders go soft because his voice is so deep and weary. I know he can't live without me.

He sits down next to me looking sheepish. I put my arm around him and nuzzle my face into his shoulder. The tears start to pour and heat fills up my chest. It's the physical feeling of love as much as I know it. I don't want an apology now. For some reason, I don't want to make him say sorry. I want him to be stronger than me and hold me, protect me from myself and that terrible belly of grief.

He pulls at me and I scoot onto his lap. He takes my head back and wipes my tears, a calloused, flat-handed wipe that feels so sweet. My nose is running, but he lets that go. I think I see tears in his eyes. We sit holding each other a long time till I grab his neck and hug him.

I pull back and grin. "I bought a gun."

Punch blinks. "You did?" He's not really smiling, but his dimple shows. He's surprised and amused.

"A .25 Beretta. Gunmetal blue. Really cute. They had a nice Colt .45, but I'm not a big-gun kinda girl."

"No?" he says. "You could have fooled me." He wipes my face again. "Where is it?"

"I didn't really buy it yet. I have to pick it up from Uncle Sam's in a few days. I just now filled out the form."

Punch chuckles. He pulls my sundress over my head and nuzzles my tits. I flatten out on the couch and he moves lower, down my stomach to the edge of my panties. I'm heating up and giggling, thinking I'm gonna get some nookie in the afternoon for a change. But he lets out a growl, pulls his head up and smooths back his hair. He stands up. "Let's go get that cycle."

The Triton costs $5,000, which is over a quarter of what we've got left for the next five months. It's the low season, but that sounds like cutting it close to me – for wild living. Punch says not to worry. We'll be having such great times on the bike we won't sit around in bars drinking five-dollar drinks. He knows what I like to hear – less drinking. Besides, he can sell the cycle for a big profit with a new paint job. The guy doesn't know what he's got.

"Apply for a couple more credit cards," Punch says. "We'll never have to pay them off anyway."

I'm hoping we'll still be around and money won't be a problem by then. But I was turned down last time I tried, so I doubt if I can get another card.

Punch rides the bike and I drive behind him. We park on Simonton and cut through to the cycle shop on Duval. I get a maroon helmet to match the gas tank and Punch gets black because he likes it, and it matches the frame. He finds a black leather vest that fits him nice, and gloves. Then he follows me home to leave the car. I snap on my shiny helmet, straddle the seat, and hunch against his back. With my legs splayed out I feel my crotch against his tailbone. I put my arms around his ribs. I'm comfortable and excited.

It's Saturday and we can't get a license plate, so we stick to the back streets. We ride all the way around the island. That long, cool, blasting salt air is enough to convince me we needed that bike after all. I guess I'm not so good at being wild. I act like a real baby sometimes.

We stop at Half-Shell for a drink and a blackened tuna dinner to celebrate, and Punch drops me home around ten. He has to show off to the guys at Tony's. I don't want to let him go while we're both still high with the newness, but I hate that place and those derelicts he thinks are his best buddies. I figure he looks at what condition they're in and feels good about himself by comparison.

I'm really down when he leaves, but I turn on the TV and *Butch Cassidy and the Sundance Kid* is on. I've watched the reruns since I was a little squirt. I never get tired of it. I could see myself as Sundance, if I knew how to shoot.

Punch does. As soon as I get my gun I'll get him to teach me.

8

◆◆◆◆◆◆◆◆◆◆◆◆◆◆◆◆◆

Punch sleeps late the next morning, but he's all ready
with part two of his plan. He tells me to dig out my jeans and
bring a jacket. We're off for the day. He's holding a piece of
cardboard that says "Lost tag 6969."

"You're not going to fool anybody with that," I say.

He shrugs.

I'm excited to go, but I realize with the bike we can't take
Bill. I walk him and feel bad, hope he has a good bladder.

Punch notices drops of oil on the blacktop under the gear
box when he starts the cycle. He sees me looking. "Nothing to
worry about. It's normal for these."

By eleven we're headed up US-1. I'm comfortable. Punch
owned motorcycles in the past and he's a good driver. Speeding
free over the bridges, I feel like a compact extension of his body
and the bike, a bullet sheering through the wind like Superman
– before his accident. Everything is puffs of meringue clouds and
miles of pure blue water. When we slow up in traffic, I can almost
pet dogs at the edge of the grass. I say hi to a couple people.
They smile back like they can tell we're taking our first ride.

We stop at Snapper's for lunch and sit on the deck out back

where it's breezy and the sun glints on the water. I order a beer, seafood and spinach stuffed mushrooms, Moscow oysters – raw, with horseradish, sour cream, and black caviar – and a crabcake with lobster sauce. Punch has a rum and coke and a cup of conch chowder.

"I'm on the light seafood diet," I tell him. "When it gets light, I see food and I eat it."

He shakes his head. "I can't figure why you don't weigh three-hundred pounds."

"Just wait. I'm working on it. Right now I'm skipping dessert, so I can still walk."

"You just have to fit on the back of the bike."

I can't quite finish the crab cake so I get a styrofoam box to take it for Bill.

"Next stop the Caribbean Club," Punch says, "the bar where *Key Largo* was filmed."

I never saw the film, but Punch always has the scoop. He says the town was called Rock Harbor until the movie. Then they renamed it Key Largo.

"That's dumb," I say.

"It's life imitating art, m' dear – sometimes a better system than the reverse. With art you can always create things the way you want them. It's tougher in life."

I wait while he cranks the bike. I know he's got his book in mind. It's a tease – he wants me to ask what he's talking about, and then he'll refuse to tell me. But I don't bite. He won't let me know anything about the novel until it's finished. All I know is that he uses our acts of craziness for inspiration. It gives him ideas instead of waiting for genius to strike. Like his artist friend. Punch told me about a guy who picks up whatever things he finds in the street each Saturday, puts felt on the bottoms, and inks them like stamps. He starts all his paintings from those shapes. Punch says they're mostly dry dog turds, but they make for realistic slices of life – they're "motifs," whatever. I said fuck

when he first told me about it – I'm no turd of inspiration. He
paid for that with hours between my legs! Even though, he never
meant it like that. I'm flattered to be a starter for Punch's
creativity.

I'm too full to feel like drinking at the Caribbean Club, but
Punch says we have to go there to celebrate the bike. Then we'll
make it to Coral Castle in Homestead, a place I've always wanted
to go.

"The bike's an adventure for both of us," he says. "We're
easy riders in the Keys." He sees I'm clueless. "It's a film. Maybe
you're thinking more like Bonnie and Clyde?" He winks. "You –
buying a gun."

I shake my head. "I never saw the movie, but I'd like to."

"We'll rent it," he says.

The Caribbean Club is on the bay side, backed up to the
water. It's a grayish building, with a bright blue awning painted
like a colorful sunset.

I feel the back of the bike skip a little as we turn into the
parking lot.

"Normal," Punch hollers. He backs the bike in next to three
other cycles, to hide the missing license. I lift my leg over the seat
and climb off. It feels good to stand. Punch looks a little stiff. I
take his arm and put it across my shoulder.

"Come on, old fart," I say. "You can make it."

He gives me a look.

In the doorway he pulls my head back by my hair and covers
my mouth in a long, open-mouthed, tongue kiss. I'm thinking I
should call him an old fart more often. I eat it up – his drama.
He puts a hand on my ass and leads me toward the bar.

It's dingy inside, dirty linoleum and dark tables, but a boxer
dog greets us and licks my hand. We sit at the bar facing an open
wall of blinding sand and water. Punch orders a rum and coke
and I get a mudslide. It's better than a chocolate milkshake and
fucking powerful.

I watch the water for a while. "I was wondering how the book's coming," I say. "I'm surprised you didn't want to work today."

He glares. I mentioned the wrong thing. I knew what I was doing, but the way he's so firm with me about letting him work makes me want to bring it to his attention that he's frittering away his time.

He looks away. "The book is wonderful," he says. His face is like rock. "It's wonderful."

I would be thrilled, except this doesn't sound like happiness. I can tell by the lack of humility what kind of a mood he's getting into. He gulps the rest of the rum and diet coke and orders a double tequila.

I know I have to distract him fast before I become the evil woman in this. "Tell me the story from the night we met. The one about the drunk."

"Not now."

"Please?"

"You'll laugh and pee your pants."

"I've never done that." I know he's trying to shut me up. "Okay. I have an idea," I say.

He stares at the beach.

"Let's take a swim."

He looks at me. I smile.

"Okay, let me finish my drink."

I'm thinking I don't have my bikini, but I need to get him away from the bar before the day is ruined.

Punch gets a go-cup, another rum and coke. We pay and walk through. "We don't have suits or towels," Punch reminds me.

Weekdays it's not too crowded, and I point right, to an empty area. "I'm going for it. I'll wear my panties."

"I wish I had my camera," he says, "in case you get arrested – g-stringed and topless in handcuffs, a couple cops in pressed shirts, bermudas and knee socks, all that against blue water. Nice. This isn't Key West, you know."

"Poop, no chance. Nobody's interested in my little titties."

We slip off our jeans. Punch has on jockeys. He always wears underwear – for zipper protection. I pull off my top and we stroll into the water. It's a little chilly. I duck down fast to get used to it. Punch squats down beside me and takes me on his lap. He fingers my nipples. They're out a mile in the chilly water. I put my head on his shoulder and enjoy his touch. Nobody's paying attention.

"You haven't put on any meat. You're built like a twelve-year-old."

I know he thinks it's a compliment, but I wish I was bigger all over.

"You love me anyway, right?" I ask.

"You're perfect."

I don't say anything and he knows what I want.

"I love you, I love you, I love you," he says.

I hug him, our chilly wet chests together, and I see over his shoulder, a cop coming our way. "I don't believe it."

He pulls back.

I point.

The cop motions us to come out of the water. "Let's let him wade in and get his shoes wet," I say.

"Come on, babycakes."

I cross my arms over my chest and follow him out. I'm hoping we aren't in for it. The Hemingway gig flashes into my brain. I wonder if we're suspects.

The cop looks at Punch's soggy briefs. He's probably thinking Punch is a ballsy black guy, planning to give him trouble. Then he sees me and stares till we're on the sand. "That your Triumph 650 with the 6969 tag out in front?" he says to Punch.

I choke on a laugh. I'm relieved it's only the license and Punch is still a little sober.

The cop looks totally serious. "There's no lost tag of that number."

Punch gets the title from his pants, since he hasn't got a registration, and gives the details about just buying the bike. He says we couldn't wait until Monday to try it out. I figure it's going to be a big fine, but okay. I turn my back and put my shirt on and yank my jeans up my wet, sandy legs. The cop writes the ticket and follows us.

I can't stop laughing on the way back through the bar. Punch just shakes his head at me.

The cop tells us to wait while he takes Punch's license over to the police car.

"He's checking my record," Punch tells me. "Don't worry. I don't have any outstanding tickets."

The cop comes back frowning. "Where you staying?"

Punch just looks at him, like it's none of his business.

"Key West," I say.

"I hope you're not planning on doing any more drinking while you're driving that bike."

I feel Punch take an attitude. "No, officer. Wouldn't think of it. I learned my lesson."

The cop hands the license back. "Take it easy," he says and walks back to his car.

I can hardly wait till he's out of ear shot. "What was all that?" I ask Punch.

"I had a D.U.I. a few years ago – got me with a breathalyzer. It's all taken care of."

He straddles the bike and I slip on behind him. "To Coral Castle," he says.

I'm pleased we're still going, but I put my hand on his arm as he reaches to turn the key. "Punch, does that mean they have your fingerprints?"

"I don't remember. I guess they must."

He feels the jolt go through me. He turns his head so I can

see his eyes. "If they had anything, we'd have heard by now. For sure this cop would have dragged me in if there was a warrant out."

I feel myself starting to shake.

"Let's go to Coral Castle. I have something to tell you. Hang on."

I know better than to ask now. I've got to ride in suspense for the next thirty or forty miles. I remind myself – nothing's good or bad, just interesting.

9

◆◆◆◆◆◆◆◆◆◆◆◆◆◆◆◆

We park in front of the concrete block tourist shop at
Coral Castle. I catch a glimpse of the rough tan coral walls amidst
the trees. I'm anxious to go in, but more interested in what Punch
is keeping from me.

I put my arms around his waist. "Can you tell me what the
secret is, so I can enjoy myself?"

"Later, darlin'." He takes off fast and I have to run a couple
steps to catch up.

Admission is seven dollars each, which I think is too much.
Punch doesn't bat an eye. He won't ruin our time by mentioning
the price, much different from my upbringing. We push the button
for the English recording and hear the weird voice that says it's
Ed. He tells how he built the castle for his sweet-sixteen girlfriend,
to lure her back after she dumped him. I already know the story
behind it from *That's Incredible* on TV.

We walk in past the ten-cent admission sign from the old
days when Ed was alive. "Wow. What percent increase is that?"
I ask Punch.

He doesn't answer. We step through the coral gate into the
courtyard. It's a much smaller area than I expected, grassy and

filled with sun-bleached carved coral in the shapes of beds, chairs,
tables, pools and fountains. Planets and a crescent moon on the
back wall rise above everything.

I go to the second recorded message and listen to Ed. He
completely followed his plan, built all of this against the laws of
gravity with the power of love. I can believe it – I know what
love will make you do. Here it is, still standing, a monument
to love, a wonder of the world forever, like the pyramids, even
though his Agnes left him. True, he was old and poor, five foot,
a hundred pounds, and sat around on hard rock day and night,
eating only sardines and crackers, but he did more for her than
any other man could have. He had unusual greatness.

The place is empty except for some kids climbing on the wall
where they're not supposed to be. I motion Punch to sit by me
on the rough bench at the heart-table. The recording says Ripley's
noted it as the largest valentine in the world at 5,000 pounds.
The ixora bush growing in the center is the same one Ed planted
fifty years ago to keep live flowers on the table for Agnes.

I want to ask Punch what he's not telling me, but I don't
dare. "Tell me the story about the drunk," I ask. "This is the
perfect place. It's the story that made me fall in love with you."

"That's ridiculous. It should have scared you away. It's embar-
rassing."

"No, it's sweet. Remember, you told me that first night?"

Punch sighs and puts his elbows on the rough pitted surface.
I snuggle under his shoulder and look up at his face. I start to
smirk already.

"I don't know why I told you this to begin with." He looks
at me. "Okay, one night Jerry and I stopped in at Windswept in
Sebastian. It was fancier than our usual hang-outs, but he liked
the wood deck on the Indian River." He stops and lifts my chin
with one finger. "You sure you have to hear this again?"

I nod. "Don't leave anything out."

He bobs his head slowly. "We'd been there a couple hours, drinking and checking out the women – "

"This was before you met me?"

He gives me a sideways glance. "Way before."

"I wonder if I was there checking out the men."

"You weren't, or I would have met you sooner. Anyway, I'm standing next to the bar waiting for a drink when this old guy falls off his bar stool and lands in a clump on the deck. Jerry helps me pick him back up, and the guy's pretty groggy. We get him on the chair and he falls off again. We pick him back up. We have to get on each side of him to walk because he's so out of it. He can't even stand.

"I drove, so I offer him a ride home and ask Jerry to help me. The man grunts something and we take him through to the front, practically falling down ourselves because he's so heavy and uncoordinated. He falls again when we try to get him into the car. Jerry and I keep looking at each other, feeling bad for the guy."

"I never met Jerry, did I?"

"No. He'd have snatched your ass right out from under me."

"Oh, man. You don't have a clue. Is he white or black?"

"A blond. You think two black guys could just waltz a white guy out of a bar in fucking central Florida?"

"You were helping him."

Punch gives me a look.

"Anyway you're mixed."

He shakes his head. "Let's see – it's at least an hour of driving around. We can barely understand the guy. We think we're going to have to take him back to the bar, but finally we manage to get the address out of him. We have to drag him out of the car and get on each side of him again. Halfway to the door, we all fall down together on the wet grass. When we stand up, Jerry's staring at me like he can't believe what I got him into. He says, 'You owe me big time, buddy.' 'Sure thing, bro,' I tell him, but I was laughing.

"We brush ourselves off and get to the door. Jerry rings the bell and we hold the guy up and wait. A woman comes to the window. She's frowning. It seems like we stand there forever, but finally the door opens. She looks left and right and then at us with a big question mark on her face. I'm thinking we've got the wrong house after all.

" 'Is this your husband?' I ask her.

" 'Yeah,' she says.

"I could see why she'd hesitate. I start to feel better, like I've done the right thing. I tell her, 'He's had a few too many, so we brought him home. His car'll be okay until tomorrow.'

" 'He don't have no car,' she says. 'Where's his wheelchair?' "

I bury my face in Punch's lap and start laughing. "You're so funny," I squeak. "I can't stand it, you're so funny." I raise up and keep laughing and holding my hand over my mouth. My jaws are starting to ache. My stomach is jumping.

"Jerry was ready to kill me. I told the woman sorry."

"You're so sweet," I whine. I try to simmer down, but tears are rolling out of my eyes. I dry them on Punch's shirt and keep laughing. My jaws are aching. "Finish it," I croak.

"We go back to the bar and, sure enough, somebody pushed the fucking wheelchair into a corner. I buy Jerry a couple shots of Jack Daniels and drive the chair to the house. I never went back to that bar again."

"I bet I would've seen that chair – I wouldn't have been that drunk. What did the woman do?"

"I don't remember. Said thanks, I guess."

I grab him around the neck. "What a dummy she was. I'd have dragged you inside and ripped all your clothes off."

"Oh yeah – I forgot to mention that part – right in front of her crippled husband."

I tap him on the cheek and he hugs me. I stop laughing and

start to feel sad because I want the good times to last forever. Real tears squeeze their way out. When times get sweet, I remember that we're planning to end it all in a few months. I can't ever be happy because my mind keeps pulling the rug out.

I wipe my eyes on Punch's shoulder. I know he can't tell the sad tears from the happy ones.

"Now that you're in a good mood, I'd better tell you the other story," he says.

I sit up straight and take a breath. I want to know this, but I don't.

"The guard from Hemingway House, um, kicked the bucket."

"Died?" I gulp for breath. "Oh, God."

"It was a freak accident. He hit his head on the midwife's chair and got a concussion. I'm not sure of the details, but he had other physical problems – high blood pressure – he was in his seventies."

"I can't believe it." I take his hand and press it on my cheek for warmth, even though it's probably ninety here in the sun. "The guy's dead?" I say again.

"I know. It's terrible. I mean it. I wouldn't have gone in there if I'd had any idea this would happen."

"When did you find out?"

"He died a couple days later."

"You knew the whole time?"

"I wasn't going to tell you. It's my problem. But when the cop ran my license, I started to think maybe you should know, in case of questions. I doubt if anything will come of it, but now there's a record of my being in the Keys. I was cautious about leaving fingerprints, just out of habit, but I'm not sure – "

"Out of habit?"

"In the past. Juvenile stuff. Cheap thrills. I was always careful to erase all the traces of myself."

"Is it murder?"

"No. Manslaughter, probably. But as I'm a black man, you never know."

"People don't think like that in Key West. That's partly why we picked it, remember?"

"Anything can happen." He looks into my eyes. "If you're thinking of us turning ourselves in, forget it. That's when everything would really get out of control."

"I feel horrible. I can't believe the guy – "

Punch nods. "It's all over. Too late to do the guard any good one way or another. We've already set our own death sentence, if you want to think of it that way. At least, I've set mine."

I sigh and lean my head on his shoulder.

"I actually bought the Triton thinking I might need a quick escape. I didn't want to worry you, so I didn't say anything. I couldn't take off with your car."

"You mean you're thinking of taking off without me?" The tears start instantly running down my face.

"No, babycakes. It's just a back-up to avoid being arrested. I might have to camp on some deserted Key for a while. You could be with me whenever you wanted."

I feel queasy. I'm holding back from getting hysterical in case other people come around. "I can't believe you never told me. That would change our whole plan. I can't believe you would just take off without me."

"It wouldn't be like that. It's just a back-up, worst case scenario. Anyway, you'd have to come live with me in the tent. We'd just have a new adventure. Spend some time outdoors – fish. I can't stand being without you for even one night."

"Now I'm scared."

"Don't be. They'd have come after me already if they had anything."

"We better get rid of that bedspread and lobster."

"We'll do that when we get home. Everything will be fine."

We look around the Coral Castle a little more, but the fun's gone. Punch says he's going to wait for me with the bike and he goes on out. I know he's probably got a flask somewhere. It's been a while since his last drink.

I walk fast to get a quick look at the rest of the place, so Punch doesn't have too much time to guzzle. I sit in the "mad rocker" Ed built for him or his sweetheart to rock off their aggression after a fight, till they felt better or got hungry. It seems like a good idea for me and Punch, but then I realize it only worked for Ed and Agnes in Ed's imagination, or else she would have stayed.

I peek into the tool shed. Ed made all his primitive tools from used car parts. Even his cook pot was a motor housing. The recording says he would broil a dozen hot dogs at a time for the kids that visited. Seems like Ed was a person who knew how to love, but never got much of a chance.

I head out to the parking lot. Punch is leaning on a tree in the shade. I give him a kiss. He's had alcohol, I think. "I'm ready," I say. "Thanks for bringing me here."

Punch turns the key and cranks the bike, but the motor doesn't catch right away. There's a big puddle under us.

"Is this from the Trojan?" I ask.

"Triton," Punch says. From his tone I can tell it was a dumb question. He motions me off and I get out of his way and go stand under the tree. He pulls a screwdriver from his pocket and I quit watching. I don't know anything about his mechanical knowledge. I hear him saying *motherfucker* and *cocksucker* over and over. Each word is like a knife through my stomach.

After about an hour Punch kicks the screwdriver into the grass and walks toward me. I'm still leaning against the tree trunk. Nobody has come by this whole time. I've been saying prayers like a kid and crossing my fingers and thumbs behind my back.

"You can't fix it?" I ask.

He stares at me and his face gets darker, if that's possible. "Can you fix it? What about you, smart-ass?"

I feel myself losing it. "Fuck!" I yell. "I didn't want it. I didn't buy it. I don't expect to know how to fix it, ass-hole!" I'm seething.

He clenches his fists and I take a breath. He lifts his hands in front of his face and his whole body shakes. He lets out a growl. Then he drops his hands to his sides, closes his eyes.

"I'm going to have to walk it about a half mile to the gas station," he says. He turns and heads toward the road, expecting me to follow.

I'm broiling with the urge to say "Cram it," but where the hell would I go. Besides I feel sorry for him. I just wish he could act like a human being, maybe think about the fact that I'm in just as much fucking trouble as he – and so much money spent on a hunk of junk.

It's after five when we get to the gas station and no mechanic on duty. Punch makes a deal with the guy to leave the bike inside the garage until the next day when he can get one of his buddies to drive up with a truck. Our choice is to take a taxi to a car rental or the Greyhound Station.

I call Greyhound and there's a bus to Key West in two hours. We go to the station and wait without saying a word. When we get on the bus, I take a seat by the window and slink down to get comfortable. I've ridden the dog before, once all the way to California and back when I visited my mother. The ride was longer than the visit.

Punch isn't speaking. I let myself fall asleep.

It's nearly eleven when we get home. Punch pulls off his clothes to take a dip and I go inside. I figure he's still got something in his flask or he'd be in for a drink. It's lucky, because Bill has pooped on the kitchen floor and walked in it. Probably didn't like being left for hours. Punch might not be in the mood to handle it. I clean up the mess fast and get all the fans going. Bill scarfs up the glob of crab cake I've been toting all day.

Punch comes in and grabs a beer. He goes into the bedroom. In a minute he walks past me in a fresh T-shirt and jeans. "I'm going out a while," he says.

"What should we do with the bedspread and lobster?"

"Later." He hits the porch and the screendoor bangs behind him.

I roll myself a joint, light it, and take a lungful. I pick up Bill and blow him a little smoke. He moves his nose aside. I feel tears wanting to come. It's been a bad afternoon and I can't take a worse night.

Punch is long gone, but I decide to take my bicycle and meet him at Tony's, much as I hate those guys. I want to make sure everything's okay between us before he's too sloshed. Then I'll head back home.

10

◆◆◆◆◆◆◆◆◆◆◆◆◆◆◆◆◆◆

The saloon is crowded and dark, with a funky smell of old and new beer. The curled, browned business cards plastered everywhere make me feel like I'm in a bat cave. I take a walk down the long rectangular wood bar. There's Punch at the end with his buddies. I know he's on the stool with Mick Jagger's name. All the stools have famous names painted in black. "Jagger" is always reserved for Punch – having to do with the song "Sympathy for the Devil," one of his favorites.

A big, red-haired barmaid is bent toward him, absorbed in whatever he's saying. Her round, peachy tits are freckled and packed perfectly into a low-cut halter top – maybe a half-inch above his glass. If he'd been drinking a white Russian, the picture could have made a great milk ad. I step up fast before she can take a breath and knock the drink into Punch's fucking lap.

I put my arm around his shoulder and the merry milkmaid straightens up. With him sitting and me standing we're eye to eye. He cuts off his conversation.

"Hi, baby," he says to me. It sounds like he's forgotten about the bike. The guy next to him gives me a short salute.

I smile at him. I can't remember his name, something odd.

"Meet Irish," Punch says and angles his chin toward the bartender and her tits. "This is Juliette."

"Nice to meet you," I say. I'm not crazy about her tits in Punch's face, but I don't feel anything against her. She's doing her job, and Punch is only flirting – he's a one-woman man. Besides, he's in a bar to drink until he can barely walk on two legs, much less get up the third.

I turn and talk into Punch's ear. "I just wanted to see how you are."

"I'm fine. You don't need to check on me."

"I just – "

"Don't worry, you hear?" He motions to the guy next to him. "Wizard is going to help me pick up the Triton tomorrow. He can probably fix it too."

"Okay."

"You going to sit down and have a drink, or go?"

Go is the key word here for me. Punch thinks I count his drinks. I can't help noticing how many, but I don't bring it up.

I'm still considering what to do until Irish asks what I'll have. "A rum runner," I say.

She moves off to mix up the fancy blender drink. Punch looks at me with his forehead wrinkled up. He nods.

I sit down next to him and all of a sudden we don't have anything to say. In a few minutes Irish brings my drink. She's holding a bottle of Bacardi in her other hand. "Want a floater?"

"Sure."

She drizzles what seems like a whole shot of rum around the frozen pink peak, plops a cherry on top, jabs a straw in the side.

"Umm," I say. It looks like a Seven-Eleven Icee, but I know it has as much liquor as three normal drinks.

Punch is shaking his head. I know he's thinking this means trouble. A couple times I got carried away on rum runners and we had a doozy of a fight. I look at him straight on. I deserve to let go on a night like this. It's his problem if he can't put up with me a little high. I do it for him everyday.

I'm thirsty and I take a big slurp. The cold goes right to my brain the first time.

I look across Punch to Wizard. "You think you can fix the Trojan?" I ask him.

Punch gives me a sideways look. He growls. "Triton."

I turn and stick my tongue out at Punch. "I sure hope so," I say. "We only took one ride."

Wizard opens his mouth to speak.

"Wiz said he can fix it, Juliette," says Punch.

I go back to my drink, hearing his tone, not really caring much about the fucking Triton. Ha. Guess Punch won't be taking off by himself for the fucking jungle. Soon I'm slurping the bottom of the rum runner.

Irish steps up. "'Nother one?"

I hand over my plastic cup.

Punch throws a look that would normally melt a hole in me, but the rum runner has put up a protective shield. I smile. Punch is in his irritable stage. I should make a list of all his moods for him.

I start sucking on my second one. It's smooth and sweet. I hear a guitar and turn to the stage. It's Skippy, another Jimmy Buffet look-alike, been here for months, but he gets his beat box going and I feel rum runner moving my legs.

"Dance with me, Punch."

"Can't dance to that shit," he says.

"Oh, please?"

He starts talking to Wizard so I take my drink and head over by myself. A few tourist couples are moving their feet and looking like it's great fun, so I take a position facing the guitarist and dance by myself, one hand on my hip, the other holding my drink. Everything's cool. I'm used to it. Punch is a much better dancer than I am, but he'll hardly ever get off his pretty ass.

I dance a while and slurp my drink. I'm feeling like the world's a happy place. Punch once told me, "Drinking is voluntary madness." I wonder where he got that, but right now I'm a happy volunteer.

Skippy announces his break and the juke box comes on loud. I start back to the bar.

"Blondie."

I turn. It's Skippy. Punch hates him, says he's a disgrace to music. Punch can barely stand being in Tony's on the nights he's playing. Skippy leans his guitar against the amplifier and catches up to me. "How ya doin?"

I just look at him.

"Ever been up on the roof?"

"No. Why would I?" I keep walking until I'm standing a short distance behind Punch. He's got Irish tits at eye level again. I bet one of those would make six of mine, but I don't give a shit.

"Let's get a drink and go up."

I look at the drink in my hand. "What's up there?"

"Peace and quiet. It's a place you can't normally go."

"Hmm." I'm always looking for a place like that. I glance at Punch. He's got three of his budds standing around.

"Hey, your boyfriend won't even notice. I see him here all the time." He motions me to follow.

Punch is absorbed, so instead of butting in I figure I'll check out the roof. If it's worthwhile, I'll bring him up. Could be a new experience for the book. "Sure it's okay?"

"Yeah. I work so cheap they give me the run of the place."

I follow him to an indentation in the front wall and he opens a door that I couldn't even see. It's plastered with old dirty and burned-looking business cards like the rest of the walls and ceiling, and it blends right in. I step over a foot high piece of doorframe into the office. I turn toward a ladder leaning next to me, but Skippy says it's broken. He shows me how to step onto a stool then boost myself to a ledge. From there I have to do a halfway pull up on my elbows to get my legs up to the next ledge and then climb through the square cut onto the scruffy shag carpet floor. What a view of my ass he's getting from below.

I stand up and we're in a dingy office with a big dusty desk and an old black telephone. It feels like trespassing so my interest is caught. "Is this where Captain Tony sits?" I ask.

He hands me my beer. "No. He doesn't own the place anymore. This is the manager's."

The next room is storage filled with boxes and piles of T-shirts. There's a big papier-mâché seahorse I recognize from last year's Fantasy Fest float. A blow-up condom that looked like a penis is deflated. I remember how much fun I had with Punch on the float showing off our skimpy costumes, Neptune and the mermaid. We had even more fun making them together.

Skippy opens a door and we step out onto the roof. There's enough light from the street, but nothing much to see – some overhanging trees, drifts of leaves, other roofs.

"Have a seat," he tells me. He points to a raised part for me to sit on the edge of the roof under branches. I sit down on crunchy leaves and tarpaper.

"That tree on the other side was a hanging tree in the pirate days," he says.

"How long ago was that?" I ask him. This would be interesting to Punch. I look at the long branches sticking out of the roof. I realize that the huge trunk in the bar below is part of this live tree. The place is built around it.

"I don't know, long time. After that the building was a morgue, then Sloppy Joe's until he moved." He puts his hand on my thigh. "Nice and cozy, huh?" he asks.

"This is where Hemingway stole the urinal, isn't it?"

"Yep."

I'm fuzzy, having over-served myself with the rum runners,

but his hand on me and the words "nice and cozy," penetrate my brain. I lean forward to stand up.

He lunges and pushes me back against the tarpaper. I smell the cigarettes in his mustache and his tongue goes into my mouth. I taste beer. I feel a rush from his warmth. His hard-on presses against my thigh through his jeans and a sweat breaks out on my back. I'm not thinking, just feeling his hand under my dress, his fingers working into my wet pussy. He pokes and digs, a little rough. I come out of my trance, and open my eyes. I don't really want him to stop. I could come in seconds, but I'm not crazy – here on the roof with this jerk and my sweetheart right below? I reach down and grab the guy's hand out of my thong.

He takes his mouth off mine. "What's the matter?"

"Gotta go. Sorry."

I stand up on wobbly legs and walk the best I can through the door and between the boxes into the office to the square hole. It's black down there, but I sit and lower myself with my arms. I know there's a board not too far. I find the ledge and hop down to the stool, then the floor. I'm feeling for the door when he lands next to me.

"Wait."

I ignore him and look into the dark, but can't get the direction.

I feel his hand on my arm. "Here." He puts a cloth into my hand. "It's a T-shirt, souvenir of Captain Tony's – and me."

"Thanks."

He opens the door. My foot catches on the bottom piece of door and I stumble into the bar and barely catch myself on a woman's shoulder.

"Awright?" she says.

I nod, but I'm looking at Punch and he's staring at me sharp as broken glass. Skippy rounds the other side of the bar and heads back to his guitar.

I straighten up and walk, but I'm wondering if my mouth looks red or if Punch can see the glaze of sex in my eyes. I notice all his budds are talking amongst themselves, turned the other direction.

"Got you a T-shirt," I say.

I glance at the tag. Lucky – it's an extra-large. I hold it up. It has Captain Tony's picture. I read: "All you need in this life is a tremendous sex drive and a great ego – brains don't mean a shit."

I laugh, but Punch doesn't. His face darkens. "What the hell is this? A fucking souvenir from the roof?" He closes his fingers around my upper arm and whispers between his teeth into my ear. "You're a cruel fucking human being."

He's in a rage and it makes me mad, especially since I didn't do anything, and now he's going to quit speaking to me again.

"You're fucking cruel," he whispers.

"I am not," I holler. "I am not. I love you and you don't care a fuck about me. You want me to sit home and watch the fucking TV while you're here pouring down the booze and having fun – and you don't even care if you kill yourself. You don't give a fuck about me."

I make a fist and plunge it into his stomach. I just want to knock some of the meanness and righteousness out of him, take his breath away so he has to pay attention to what I'm saying.

He makes a noise of surprise. I pull back for another hit, but he grabs my wrist and turns it behind my back. I use my other hand to try to pull his arm away, but he gets a hold of it too. My little finger is pushed up. It bends backward.

I try to wrench away but he holds tight. We're both drunk and clumsy and in a second I hear a pop and feel a singeing pain run from my little finger up my arm.

I start crying. "You hurt me! You hurt me, you bastard!"

He lets go and shakes his head like to wake up.

I hold out my hand. It's shaking and the little finger is hanging at an angle. I'm almost glad it looks bad, except it hurts so much. Now there's something real to show him so he'll feel sorry.

I keep my shaking hand out and stare at his face. I want him to feel terrible. Somewhere in the back of my head I have a tiny speck of hope that something could make him feel bad enough to stop drinking.

Punch lightly takes my hand and lifts it close to his face. He doesn't say anything, but tears fill up his eyes and run down. All the budds are watching. He turns back to the bar and takes a long drink of his rum. He sets it down and slumps. His head drops to his folded arms and he knocks his drink over with his elbow. He doesn't even move out of the puddle.

I turn and run to the door. I don't know what to do but I don't want to stand there and cry in front of his friends. I get to Duval and start running toward home, holding my finger against my chest to keep it from bouncing.

In less than a block my stomach is queasy. I stop. I don't have much choice and I hunch over the gutter and let the pink juice splash into the street. I feel the spray on my ankles and between my toes in the flip-flops.

When I straighten up I'm lightheaded. I step back and lean against a glass storefront. I feel weak and my hand is throbbing. I'm at Angela Street. I look around the corner and see the low picket fence that runs along the front of the witch shop. The stores are all closed by now, but I wonder if Isis is still up. I'm thinking I could sit in her kitchen and have a cup of tea. Maybe she knows something to make my hand feel better. Then I can go back to Tony's and get my bike.

I walk the few doors down. I see a light inside so I go to the door and knock. In a few seconds Isis looks through the window. She's surprised but opens right up.

"I'm sorry. I was just passing by. I hurt my finger."

She puts her hand on my shoulder and moves me inside, leading me to a chair in the kitchen.

She takes my hand lightly in hers. "The finger's dislocated," she says. "I'll drive you to the hospital."

"It's too much trouble. I just want to sit a few minutes and have tea."

"Where's your boyfriend?"

I wave the question aside. "I'll call a taxi, if I can just use your phone."

"No. I'll take you."

I give in. "Okay, I guess." The pain is overwhelming.

She gets her bag and leads me out to the car. In the hospital waiting room, she asks me what happened. I know she's going to think I'm a total basket case, but I guess I need some sympathy. I tell her Punch did it accidentally. We both had too many drinks and got into a fight. He didn't mean to hurt me.

She shakes her head like she could have guessed I'd be that dumb, but she doesn't say a thing. The nurse takes me in and I'm glad I don't have to talk about it anymore.

On the way home I'm really groggy from the pain pill they gave me. I look at my hand with the finger wrapped to a metal holder down the side. The pain's still throbbing, even worse since the doctor pulled it back into place. I have to keep the splint on for a month. At least I have something to show Punch when he's sober in the morning. I want a "sorry" this time. I want him to see what his drinking causes.

"Could you drop me home?" I ask Isis. "I'll walk back for my bike tomorrow."

"Okay," she says.

I open my eyes and we're parked on the street near the witch shop. Isis has the passenger door open. She touches my arm.

"Come on. I didn't want to wake you. You can spend the night here. I have an extra room."

"No, I have to go home," I tell her. "Punch won't know what happened to me."

"He should have thought about that before he dislocated your finger. Let him worry."

"It wasn't his fault. I can't."

"I'll take you home early in the morning. He's not going to wait up worrying if he's as drunk as you say."

As much as I wish it isn't true, I know she's right. He might not even remember what happened, just zonk off to sleep in the chair – wearing his contacts. I don't really feel like leaving for a night of misery, waiting for him to get home and then not talking. As long as I'm back before he gets up, he'll never miss me. Bill might run out, but I figure he'll be okay inside the compound.

I follow Isis up the stairs through wispy curtains into an atmosphere of incense. I see a satin bedspread and glowing candles as we pass her bedroom and step into a small dark room. She snaps on an orange lava lamp that glows just enough so I don't fall over a chair.

"The next door down is the bathroom. Clean towels in the cupboard if you want a shower."

She walks out and I look around. The bed has an antique-looking spread that reminds me I still have to get rid of Hemingway's. I pull it down and the sheets are beautiful with seashells and pink embroidery. They look brand new.

I decide to take a shower before crawling into them. I go into the bathroom and pull off my dress. It's a chore with one working hand. The splinted one is still pumping like hell. I see my horrible face in the mirror, all puffy from crying and drinking. I'm feeling nervous about spending the night with a lesbian. I wonder what it would be like for her to touch my body, if she's thought of licking inside me. I look at myself again in the mirror, dark skin under my eyes, my stringy hair. How could I think Isis would be attracted to me? That's something about Punch – he never notices my flaws.

I manage to keep my hand out of the shower, wrap myself in a fluffy towel, and go back to my room. The lava lamp is circulating red amoeba shapes. I consider shutting the door, but Isis might think I'm afraid of her coming in. I hang the towel over a chair and climb into the cool sheets. This is the first night I've slept without Punch since we've been together.

I close my eyes and my hand starts shooting fire again. I try to get comfortable, but I can't quit hurting and worrying about Punch. I get up, pull my dress over my head, and walk quietly down the hall to Isis' room. I don't want to wake her, but if she's still up, I plan to ask her to take me home.

In the hall I smell cinnamon and apples, taste something minty on my lips. Her door is open. I look to the far right and freeze. She's naked, her back to me, kneeling in the middle of a circle painted on the wood floor. Leaves and powder are sprinkled around the circle between a dozen or more burning pink and green candles. She's speaking softly with her head bowed. My eyes are magnetized by the shine of her perfect white skin in candlelight, the long slimness of her back, every muscle and bone visible to her thin waist. Before I can move away, she turns and stands.

I haven't seen such a tall, sleek woman's body before. Her eyes are in the shadows of her high cheeks, and her delicate shoulders, collarbones, and ribs make her look breakable as a china figurine. Her hair is hanging forward, wispy over her small tits with tiny points of dark nipples. My eyes draw over her flat stomach to the black pointed beard of her bush.

I catch my breath. "I'm sorry," I say. "My hand hurts and I wanted to ask you to take me home."

She slowly puts her finger to her lips then motions me toward her. It's spooky, but I'm curious about what she's doing. I don't believe in this stuff, so it can't hurt. I step over the circle and face her. I'm not used to being this close to a naked woman, but she's looking through me to some far-off place, and it isn't a come-on. She lifts my dress and I put my arms up and let her take it off. She throws it on a chair outside the circle. "Wait a minute," she says.

I wait there naked while she blows out the pink and green

candles and gets some white ones to replace them with. "I was preparing another spell, but it's more important right now to do a healing for your pain."

Her eyes get shiny and she puts her palms over my head and closes her eyes. She keeps the position for some time and then opens her eyes and moves down to my forehead, pauses, then to my neck. Her fingers are a hair's width from my skin. I hold my breath as she gets to my nipples, but they rise with a chill and graze her fingertips. She has her eyes closed and doesn't seem to notice.

I can't help wondering what her mouth would feel like on my skin, her hands cupping my tits. My chest tingles and goose-bumps rise on my arms. She moves down to my stomach then above my crotch. I think what the sensation would be of her fingers parting my lips, her tongue slipping inside me. I feel the wetness cool between my thighs and I keep my legs tight together.

Next, she takes the hand with the finger and repeats Psalm 27 three times – no matter how hard I try to forget it, the Bible always comes back to me.

"Under grace and for the good of all, may the Goddess grant that Juliette's pain be taken away," she says. She kneels and gives thanks.

A tingling runs all the way down me.

She looks up. "All finished." The words are soft and she smiles. She stands and moves toward the chair to hand me my dress and grab a blue robe.

I fumble to pull my dress on. She ties the silky robe around her with a sash, lifts her hair from under the fabric. "Believe in it. It will work." She lifts my injured hand and rests it on her palm. "How do you feel?"

"Some better," I say. "I forgot about it." I'm thinking it's just the strangeness of doing her weird ritual, and as soon as I lie back down the fire will start again, but I still feel a tingle. Anyway, I don't want to disappoint her. "Thanks. I appreciate it."

"It will heal fast. Now let me relax you." She starts moving her fingers lightly up and down my arm, turning her wrist gracefully to make loops that move upward to my shoulder. The sensation is soothing. "I'm trained in massage," she says.

I feel myself relax and the pain goes away more, but I don't know if it's magic. I always like being stroked. I don't want her to stop.

She works up to my neck and lifts my hair. Her fingers start working into my scalp and I let my head loll on my chest. I could fall asleep on my feet.

"Come over here."

I hesitate because she's motioning to the bed, but her fingers have stopped and I want them to start again.

"I'm not going to touch you sexually," she says.

I take a breath. Waves of chills have moved from her fingers into every part of my body until I'm weak. I feel a drip running down the inside of my thigh.

I trust her – if not myself – and walk to sit on the bed where the ruffled sheet is neatly turned down. It's so nice. I'm not used to made beds.

"Lie on your stomach," she says.

I lift the sheet and slide under to my waist and lie flat with my face toward her.

She positions my arm so it's comfortable at my side and sits next to me on the edge of the bed. She bends and starts massaging my shoulders again. The waves roll over me and I breathe sighs of pleasure.

"You're a dove," she says. "You coo like a dove and you have the pure beauty." She smiles down at me.

"It feels great," I tell her.

I close my eyes and relax heavier into the bed. Her fingers press alongside my backbone and fuzzy, warm sleep comes over me. I open my eyes to tell her I'd better go to my room. Her robe is hanging open. Her breasts are inches from my face as she's bent over me. They look so soft – like pets – I want to hold them. I think of their weight like my own and the feeling of touching myself. I want her hands on me. I want to press my face into her white breasts. I close my eyes.

I wake up facing a window, sunlight coming in across the bed. I have to think where I am and it gives me a nervous start. I turn to see if Isis is sleeping next to me. She's not. I'm taking up most of the bed. I can't tell if she's been there.

I get up and put my dress on. My hand is feeling much better, and I don't even have a headache like I would expect from the rum runners. I'm a little off balance, but I know I have to get home to Punch fast.

I walk through the store and stop to pet the short-tailed black cat sitting on a chair. She stands and rounds her back into my hand. I remember I'm in a hurry and walk into the kitchen. Isis is still in her robe, making tea. "Can I fix you something to eat? I have oatmeal or homemade grain bread."

The bread tempts me. "No, thanks. I've got to get going. Punch will go crazy worrying if he wakes up and I'm not there."

"A good reason to stay," Isis says. "He should have thought about the consequences last night." She stops pouring. "Sorry. I shouldn't have said that."

"It's okay."

She hands me a cup of tea and dries her hands. "Let me throw on some clothes and I'll drive you."

I hold up my hand and stroke the finger. "It doesn't even hurt this morning. I guess you fixed me." I look at her bright morning eyes. "My bike's just around the corner. It'll be easier if I just get it and ride home."

She steps close and looks hard at me. "You sure?"

I break the stare and glance down. I see the cleavage of her breasts, smooth mounds under the blue silk. "I'm almost good as new. Thanks for everything."

"Listen, I can't let you ride off like that," she says. "I have to rush this morning, but I'm going to call Twig to get you in her taxi. She can take your bicycle too – do you know her? She does Frank Sinatra impersonations."

I shake my head no.

"She's a character." She lifts my chin with her fingertip. "You're welcome here anytime you want – for a cup of tea, or to spend the night, as long as you need to stay if you're in trouble."

"Okay," I say. I feel myself blushing. I'm embarrassed at how I came here and let her massage me, even spent the night in her bed, but I still feel comfortable around her. I'm thinking how Punch had the idea of taking off without me on the Triton. It feels good to have somebody else I can trust. "Thanks. I need a friend," I tell her. I feel the urge to give her a hug and I do it. I'm awkward and almost knock her over, but she steadies us both and hugs back.

She calls the taxi and when it stops outside, Isis follows me to the door. I'm walking fast, anxious to get home to Punch, and still feeling ungrateful. I turn and try to give her my hand in the splint. She takes my arm and pulls me forward gently in a hug. Her warm lips touch my forehead.

I pull back. "Thanks again. I don't know what I can do for you, but – ?"

She shakes her head. "We're friends. You would help me if I asked you."

"Sure," I say. "Anytime." Instantly I'm wondering what I can do for a lesbian witch, but I trust her. She must know she could have done anything she wanted with me already.

"Give me your phone number. I want to call later and see how you are."

I give it and she says she'll remember. I wave from the sidewalk.

I step into the taxi and tell Twig where to get my bicycle.

When we get there, she lifts the bicycle into the trunk easily, then makes a muscle. "Fifty push-ups every morning," she says.

She ties down the trunk and nods back toward the witch shop. "Isis is a special person," she tells me. "Unusual."

The way she says it, I know she means something about the magic. I want to ask more, but I can't find the right question.

I feel like a ninny for not riding home. I look at my splinted finger. It's part my fault, but Punch better be real sorry. He better be.

11

◆◆◆◆◆◆◆◆◆◆◆◆◆◆◆◆◆

I step onto the porch at our cottage. I hear Punch in the kitchen banging dishes into the sink. It sounds louder than it needs to be. There's part of a joint in the ashtray and I light it up, take three good hits before I open the door.

He looks up as I walk inside. Then he looks back down at a skillet he's washing. "Too late for breakfast," he says.

I can't tell if he's controlling his voice, but it sounds like a dangerous understatement to me. I come up next to him and cross my arms with the splinted finger on top.

He sees it from the corner of his eye and jerks. He turns toward me with a sponge dripping on the floor. "What's that?"

I can tell he doesn't remember. I start to cry. I thought all this time he was thinking how bad he hurt me.

"What did you do?"

I sob out my rendition of the crazed night, leaving out the details of my trip to the roof, so not to sidetrack the whole story. I make sure he understands all about the pain and the hospital and that I spent the night with a lesbian witch because I was too hurt to get myself home.

When I'm finished he's hanging his head. I can tell from his face he recognizes enough to know I'm telling the truth.

"I know I shouldn't drink rum runners," I tell him, "but I get lonesome when you go off with the guys. I want to have fun too. We're supposed to be doing crazy things together."

"Poor babycakes," he says. "I didn't mean to hurt you. I never want to. It almost kills me when I hurt you." He picks up my hand and kisses it and hugs my face into his clean T-shirt. He puts his arm around my shoulder and walks me to the couch.

Bill is on the end cushion and we sit together next to him. I reach across with my good hand to stroke Bill's shiny head. "Has he been out this morning?"

"Of course." Punch puts his arm around me and tilts his head against mine. "Tell you what," he says. "I have to take a ride to Key Largo to pick up the bike. It's the only day Wiz has time. You stay here and rest. When I get back, we'll go to a twilight movie and then wherever you want to eat. Just like you like."

It sounds so nice, a cool theater and buttered popcorn. He knows I love the movies. It's especially true because they don't serve alcohol and then we get to talking afterwards. Punch notices interesting stuff that I miss. We discuss film techniques and symbolism.

But I can't get happy. Late afternoon is so far off and in between Punch is going all the way to Key Largo with Wizard. It's another writing day shot – two in a row – and I know he won't make it back sober.

"I could ride along," I say.

"It would be too crowded in his pick-up. Besides, you'd be bored." He looks at my watery eyes. "Listen, babycakes, I don't ever want to spend another night apart. I thought you left me. I think I would have fucking killed myself by tonight if you hadn't come back."

I know he's serious. Life doesn't mean much to him. Just like for me – without each other there'd be no reason to hang on.

"Please don't forget to come home in time."

He looks stung. "It was my idea. I'm not going to forget."

He's in a hurry to go. He finds his wallet and shoes. "I'm meeting the Wiz outside the gate. Look in the paper for something around five."

"We still have that bedspread and lobster," I remind him.

"We'll take them somewhere later – after midnight."

He leaves and I try to settle myself down. I know he means what he says. He really thinks we'll make it to the movies. I'm not a baby, after all. If we don't get to go, it's not gonna kill me. I check the paper, one theater with a bunch of screens. James Bond at five-thirty is the only possibility.

I try napping and can't. I walk around in the pool with my splinted hand up, but it's no fun. I'm not having a wild time in Key West. I call Uncle Sam's and the guy says I can pick up my gun.

As I pay for the Beretta, I'm already starting to feel better. When I get home I sit on the couch next to Bill and roll myself a big joint, inhale deeply. I'm much better. I admire the compact design of the gun and sit for a long time feeling the way my hand conforms to the grip. I line the bullets up on the coffee table in a semi-circle in front of the Beretta, so Punch will see it whenever he comes home.

I lie back to rest with Bill. I'm thinking now that I have my gun I need to go flashing again. I remember I never told Punch about the first time. I drift.

I dream I'm zooming across the seven-mile bridge holding onto Punch on the Triton. But the road's gone and there're just two strips for car tires and we're riding on one. We follow turns and twists like a roller-coaster. It ends. We shoot off and drop down, down, through a tangle of moray eels swirling on the surface of the water.

I'm still holding onto Punch and the Triton pulls us down deep. Finally he lets go of the bike and it disappears into blackness. I grab Punch's arm and try to pull him back up, but he's not helping. I feel the foam and currents from boat propellers on my legs. I croak a tiny help in the back of my throat.

I float to the beach at Bahia Honda. I trudge up the slope of sand and there's Punch, flat out in the edge of the surf, gleaming in sunlight. It's like we're in a movie. He opens his eyes. I can feel the kissing and his hands in my hair, his warm wet skin on mine, his hard cock sliding into my body. I know he'll never take another drink.

I open my eyes feeling good, then sad, because it's a fantasy. I don't want to dwell on it. I move Bill off my lap and go to the kitchen for a beer. It's already five-thirty. The phone rings. I think, well, at least Punch is sober enough to call. But it's Isis. She wants to know if I'm feeling okay and if things were straightened out with Punch. I tell her everything's fine and she repeats her offer for me to stop over. I take a rain check.

I know by now I'm not going to a movie, so I snap on the Food Channel and roll another joint – no pouting. We've had enough trouble in the last couple days.

It's my turn for an idea, so I start thinking about what would be interesting. Pop comes to mind. "Don't tell me you're bored," he used to say when I was a kid. "If you can't think of something to do in this world, it's your problem – you're boring." He'd come up with a chore, like picking up leaves. That's when my mom was still around. I learned young not to be bored, even before he started his little "punishments" and "purifications."

I remember the lobster plaque and bedspread stuffed in the closet. Tonight I'm going to get rid of them whether Punch is in condition to help or not. I watch Paul Prudhomme fry softshell crabs and think I should get some fresh ones and try it. I had an uncle who was a chef and I remember him making them for me and Pop one time. I thought about going to chef school, but there wasn't one close by. Pop said I could learn the same thing from recipe books, but it wasn't the same. I just kept an interest in eating.

Punch wanders in at dark and he's so bedraggled, I don't even feel mad. He tells me the motorcycle needs a new engine. I don't get a clue about what's wrong with it, except it's bad, but I let it drop and ask if he's eaten. He says he had a burger. He goes to take out his contacts and in a minute I hear him snoring in the bedroom.

I set my clock-radio for two a.m. and curl up with my foot against his calf for a few hours sleep. I don't want to make us sweat, but I need some touching, whatever I can get.

Punch rolls over and keeps snoring when the alarm goes off. I want to go back to sleep, but I have to do what I planned. I throw on a dark dress and my black wig and put the bedspread and lobster in a big green garbage bag. I don't have any dark jeans because I left my only pair the last time. I figure I'll heave the bag over the fence and take off.

I drive the car and park it on Olivia for a fast getaway. I look around and take the bag from the passenger side, cross the sidewalk and look over the fence. I want a spot under a bush or something. I see a table. Maybe the police will think the bag was left there all along, no theft involved. It's awkward with my splint, but I lift the bag over the fence. There's garden stuff blocking the view from the other side. I lower the bag carefully, lobster side up, and flap the top over in case of rain.

I look around – still nobody there – and step into the street behind the car. I nearly stumble over a cat. The dark fur blends with the pavement and the animal doesn't move. I think for a second it's dead and I ran over it. It whimpers and I look close. The eyes are open wide and scared. There seem to be drops of blood on the concrete. I don't know what to do. I lift a paw. Sure enough, it's a six-toed. I can't ring the bell and give it to the guard, or when they find the stuff, they might connect me. I can't let the cat suffer in the street all alone.

I think of Isis – shit, another favor I'm asking. I don't know anything else. Punch claims to like animals better than people, but he wouldn't know what to do. I get a towel out of the back seat and scoop the cat up easy. He doesn't try to get away, so he's either real tame or almost dead. I put him on the seat and drive to Isis' place.

The lights are out so I knock hard. She's sleepy when she opens the door, but wakes up fast when she sees what I'm holding. She motions me to bring it into the kitchen and lay it on the table. The cat is a pretty gray tabby with a white spot on the chest. The blood's seeping from the shoulder.

Isis gets some antiseptic and a clean cloth and dabs at the wound, feels around and moves the leg. "It's not broken. I need to apply a herb mixture to stop the bleeding." She motions me next to her. "Keep pressure on this until I'm ready."

I hold the folded bandage in place and wait.

She brings a mortar and pestle that looks ancient. She grinds something, makes a paste with water, applies it to the cat's shoulder, and holds the bandage over it.

"This is a Hemingway cat," she says. "Or a relative of one."

"Uh huh."

"Where'd you find it?"

"In the street. At first I thought I hit it. I couldn't think where to take it so late."

"In front of your house?"

"No. I was out."

She frowns and I know she's thinking I shouldn't be out alone at three in the morning. I want to explain, but I can't. She doesn't ask any more questions. She checks the wound. "It's stopped. I'm going to wrap it up with some herbs and hope it – " She checks between the legs – "hope she doesn't pull it off. She'll be fine in a day or two – lucky."

"Can she stay here till then?"

"Of course, but somebody's probably looking for her."

I nod. "I'll knock on some doors tomorrow."

I thank her for bailing me out again. "If you did as well on the cat as on me, she'll be better by morning," I tell her.

"I hope now you understand more about the meaning of witchcraft," she says. "My purpose is to help those who ask, in any way I can – for the good of all." She gives me a hug and a kiss on the forehead, which I guess is going to be a habit. "Get some sleep," she says. "I'll talk to you tomorrow."

12

◆◆◆◆◆◆◆◆◆◆◆◆◆◆◆◆◆

I wake up at noon and Punch is hard at work on the computer. He has the TV turned low. I never even heard him get up. I'm naked as usual and I walk over and kiss him and hug his curly head to my bony chest. His face is warm and soft on my body.

"Your breakfast is in the refrigerator," he says. "And I already took Bill out. You okay?"

I'm not sure if Punch is going to be happy with the cat situation, and I don't want to interrupt his writing, but I sit down on the couch, pick up Bill, and blurt out the whole story.

He turns on the swivel chair and looks at me with his eyebrows up.

"I didn't want to bother you with taking that stuff back. I was getting real nervous. I couldn't leave that cat in the street."

"Come here."

I put Bill on the floor and think, oh shit. I don't need a lecture. I walk over and stand facing him.

He picks up my hands, the normal one and the one with the Nightmare-on-Elm-Street finger. "Darlin', don't worry. Everything's fine. Just don't give too much information to your friend

the witch, just in case. We don't want to waste our time with the
law if we can help it."

"Isis is nice. She wouldn't get me in trouble."

"I'm sure." He grins. "You two been doing a little licking and
sucking over there at the witch house?"

"No! Punch!"

"Don't get so excited. I was just asking. It's no big deal."

"Well, I'm not doing anything," I say. A guilt pang hits me –
I thought about doing something.

"That's fine. I'm glad you have a friend. Just don't tell her
any of our business, okay?"

"Promise."

I'm so horny right then I forget he's trying to work on the
book. I slide onto his lap with my legs on both sides of his hips,
my arms around his. I feel the heat radiating up my body. I move
a handful of salt and pepper hair and kiss his soft brown neck.

"Okay," he says. "Later. Okay?"

I pry myself off and sneak one last kiss on his ear. I go and
sit in the chair in front of the TV to cool down. The news is on.
I can't believe it – a newsman again at the Hemingway House.
They already found the bag.

Punch looks over. "Uh oh," he says.

The reporter does a recap of our story, adding the new devel-
opments. "Now there's a Hemingway cat missing," he says. "One
might wonder with sixty-some cats, how anybody would know,
but each morning this particular cat – named Moon-cat, for a
white crescent on her chest – greets the tour guides at the gate.
When she didn't appear today, employees searched the grounds,
turning up the missing items – but no Moon-cat. It's believed the
stolen goods were returned last night, since landscape workers
didn't notice the bag earlier when planting in the area. Possibly
the same person or persons who returned the bedspread and
lobster have the missing cat."

"How can they be sure she was taken? She could be anywhere."

"But they're right, aren't they?" says Punch.

I feel shaky, but I don't want him to know. "She'll be better in a couple days and I'll return her. They'll think she was hiding."

Punch rolls his eyes at me and I go on outside. I pull my dress off and swim in my thong panties. In a while Punch comes out. He's got a drink for himself and one for me. "I can't write fucking shit today," he says. He sits on the chaise lounge and wipes his face with his hands.

I sit on the chair next to him. "You need a jump start," I say. "I can help you." I hold my tits out to him.

He taps one nipple and lets his hand fall. "I'd be happy if I could get one good page."

"Tell me a story. Maybe that'll get you going."

"I can't think." He gulps his rum.

"Tell me about the night you spent with that woman – in Gatlinburg."

"I told you that?"

"Two times. I like how you tell it. The details change."

He frowns, stretches out on the lounge, and puts his hands behind his head. I look at his muscles and my eyes slide over his chest and past his belly-button down the little trail of hair that runs into his bathing suit.

I put my hand on his arm. "Come on, please?"

"Okay. The short version." He closes his eyes. "I met this woman in a bar – she was white, with a butterfly tattoo on her right tit and both nipples pierced. Not generally my type, but this was fifteen years ago when these things were unusual – "

"Want me to get a tattoo? A little salamander crawling up my hip?"

Punch looks me over. "No. Definitely not."

"Pierced nipples?"

He shakes his head. "Forget it. You're perfect like you are.

Anyway, she took me to this cabin where she was staying and we were drunk and carrying on. I didn't even know where I was really, somewhere in the tourist area. Pine trees and mountain peaks out the window."

"Was the sex good?"

"I don't remember."

"Sure," I say. "I think we better go make some memories so you can take notes."

"You have a one-track mind."

I run my fingers down his ribs. "Go on."

"Anyway, I wake up in the middle of the night and have to piss. I open the door across from the bed and it's a kitchen with a light on. I walk through looking for the bathroom. I turn into a hall and a big white guy steps in front of me. He's naked too.

" 'Fuck!' he yells.

" 'Fuck!' I yell.

"We're standing there face to face. I remember feeling like I didn't know what to do with my arms.

"I ask him, 'Who the fuck are you?'

" 'The fuck are you?' he says. 'Get your gay ass outta my house!'

"Did you have a hard-on?" I say.

"Fuck no. But I had a bladder full of piss. I say, 'Hey, man, I was invited. I'm sorry if she's your old lady, but I'm in a hurry to find the john.'

"He's stunned. He gets a weird look and moves aside, and I see the pisser right in front of me – that's where he came from. I go in and take care of business and when I come out he's zipping up his jeans. 'So where the fuck's my old lady?' he says. 'I haven't seen her for a month.'

"I'm thinking this is real strange. 'She's still in bed, I guess.'

" 'You're a fucking lunatic, man. She ain't here.'

"I motion him to follow me and he walks with his mouth hanging open. I'm curious to hear her explanation. He follows me into the kitchen and we open the door. There she is in the light spilling onto the bed, sleeping there, shining naked.

"She sits up and looks at us. 'Oh, no. Fuck, no!' she yells. 'I'm not up for this. Get this loser out of here.'

" 'Sorry, man,' he says. 'Really. I don't know this chick. These are rentals. This door should have been locked.'

"I just shrug. I figure I was lucky not to be shot. We laugh like nuts, and the woman stares at us. I spot the real bathroom door in the corner.

"He and I met at the bar the next day and never stopped laughing, became good friends."

I'm thinking it was the booze causing all the trouble, as usual, and still it ends up number one on the day's plan. "Men and bars," I say. "Did you screw the woman again?"

"No, m' dear. I left town."

"Seems like you used to be more easy-going when you drank."

"Shit. I'm too easy-going now." He motions with his glass. "Speaking of which – I'm ready for another drink. You?"

I put my feet on his thigh. "I just thought of the time I made a prank call."

"*You* made a prank call?"

"In high school. I had a crush on this boy, but was too scared to talk to him, you know? I'd dial and hang up. Only – one time my father picked up the extension just when the guy answered. He said, 'Hello.' Pop said, 'Hello? Hello?' The boy said, 'Hello?' Pop said, 'Hello.' I was dying – trying not to laugh and being scared to death at the same time, thinking they'd both find out what I did. Finally they hung up. Unlucky for me, Pop figured out later I was on the other line, fooling around. I caught hell."

"What did he do?"

"I don't know – probably whacked me and gave me an enema or something."

"An enema?"

"To clean me out, you know – purify." My face gets hot. "I

forget. Let's go inside. I'll fix us a drink. Then I want to lick you all over."

He scoops me up and I love it. He nuzzles his face in my little tits and carries me in. I go to the kitchen to make the drinks.

When I walk into the bedroom, he's stretched out on the bed, his long caramel body tempting as an ice cream sundae, waiting for me. I hand him his drink and crawl up him, stroking his legs with my fingers and tongue, drawing my splint lightly behind his knees for a new feeling.

"Your father gave you enemas? How old were you?"

I kiss his thigh. "I don't know. He always did it. I thought it was normal. He had this orange rubber bag with a long tube."

I move to his groin. "I'm done talking. I need to use my mouth for other purposes." I lick inside his thighs and take his soft balls into my mouth and then his cock. I get him hard and slide down on top of him, but it doesn't last. I can't even keep him inside. The tears come because I want him there so bad. He moves me off and goes down between my legs. I feel his fingers exploring my folds and then his tongue takes up the regular rhythm. He only wants to please me. I flow into it. I tighten up hard and then let it all out.

He starts up again and I get another come in no time. He's real tender and kisses my pussy afterward. He turns me over and kisses my ass and takes my cheeks apart. I feel his tongue prod in between, then his finger real gentle, poking. I think of his face above me, his eyes searching my most hidden spots and thinking they're beautiful.

I know he's picturing me in the bathroom, draped across Pop's lap with my panties down, Pop guiding that long tube between my cheeks and filling me up, then holding me so I can't get up to relieve myself.

Punch wets his finger and keeps me going. He puts it farther inside me and a tingle spreads through my whole body. My muscles tighten and I twitch with the rushes of coming. After-

wards he strokes down my back using his fingertips to relax me.
I'm wondering if he's going to try to put his cock in back, but he
turns me over and gets on top. He's hard as rock and I know it's
from thinking of me with Pop, but I don't care. He keeps it up
long enough till I shudder and come again. His face contorts and
he comes inside me and I feel his love fill up my whole body. I
can't remember the last time he did that.

I wake up hearing him in the living room, tapping away at
the computer. I feel good. I fall back to sleep.

When I get up Punch says get ready for dinner. I tell him Bill
wants to go to the restaurant, but Punch says let's not. He's not
in the mood to be blind. He says we need to go somewhere
reasonable because we're running a little ahead of our budget.
He's applied for credit cards, but they haven't come yet. He also
needs some bucks to fix the Triton if he's going to get our money
back out when he sells it.

I'm glad he's talking about selling the Triton, but I'm feeling
pissed that we have to scrimp now. The phone rings and Punch
answers and hands it to me. It's Isis. I tell her I'm leaving to go
eat. I'll call afterward.

"We could stop over together," I tell Punch. "She's interesting
– for the book."

"We'll see."

We stop at an outside cafe on Duval where it isn't cheap, but
Punch says he knows a waiter. "I think he'll give us a deal," he
says. "I'm not that hungry anyway."

"We could have brought Bill here outside," I say. I'm still
pissed and also starving. I doubt Punch's friend is going to give
us a discount. "Maybe we could limit our drinks?"

The hostess comes up to seat us and Punch asks for Monty's
section. I recognize the name.

Punch and Monty shake hands and Punch explains we're a
little short on cash. Monty whispers to us that the soups and

salads are free to special customers tonight. If we order one entree and drinks, everything's cool.

"Thanks, buddy, I owe you," Punch says.

We order a rum with diet coke and a margarita, and Monty goes off to get them.

I feel embarrassed. I look at the menu. "It's still not going to be that cheap with drinks."

"Let's not worry about it."

I give him my exasperated look, but he ignores it. "Is that the Monty you got the key from? For Hemingway's?"

"Yeah. He hasn't been at Tony's lately. I just heard he was working this job – odd, him as a waiter."

We each get a soup and salad and I order a pasta primavera. Punch says he has plenty to eat.

We're nearly finished when a dark-haired guy wrapped in a pearl and yellow python and holding a bright green, five-foot iguana with a pink bow around its neck runs up to the entrance. The guy's sweaty and out of breath. I recognize him from sunset on Mallory Dock. He takes pictures with the tourists.

The hostess is standing on the sidewalk watching him. "Take him and run!" he yells. He throws the iguana into her arms. "Take Iggy and run!"

Behind him a big man is catching up, dodging tourists on the sidewalk. He's hollering fuck again and again. "I'll get you, you motherfucker!" he screams.

Without Iggy, the snakeman takes off fast. "I'll pick him up later," he calls back. The hostess is struggling to keep the iguana from crawling over her shoulder. It makes its way into her long hair and stops, tangled up with its nails and spines. She starts to walk then freezes. The big man runs past her.

I start to get out of my chair and Punch grabs my arm. "We can't keep a fucking iguana," he says.

"I'm just gonna help."

"You've done enough good Samaritaning for a while."

I shake off Punch's hand and start to move, but the hostess grabs the iguana's back to keep it from squirming and walks toward the inside.

I turn and walk back to the table.

"She's taking it to the chef," Punch says. He points to the list of specials on a blackboard. "We'll see an addition there in a minute."

I'm laughing. "Punch, that's awful! I love iguanas."

"Just funning in Key West, darlin'."

His good Samaritan comment reminds me of the cat. It dawns on me that Isis might have heard the news report and started to wonder.

I ask Punch if he thinks Monty might know what's going on about the Hemingway thing. We order another drink and Punch and Monty whisper. Monty goes off.

"Well?"

Punch frowns and sets his jaw. "He heard the police got some prints – yours – from the bathroom." He throws down the rest of his drink. "But don't worry. There was a party earlier that week. They think somebody could have gone up there then. They really don't have a thing."

I'm not feeling so confident. It seems like details are stacking up against us.

Punch pays a twenty-dollar check and leaves a five-dollar tip. We thank Monty and walk out. I know I shouldn't worry so much. Like Punch says, the justice machine moves slow. My middle-class conscience is ruining the short time we have left, if that's the way it's going. Nothing's good or bad, just interesting – or boring, if I let it be.

13

◆◆◆◆◆◆◆◆◆◆◆◆◆◆◆◆

Punch opts for Tony's and I go alone to see Isis. When she comes to the door I'm glad Punch is gone because her face tells me she's figured it all out. She's in that satiny blue robe again and I wonder if she ever wears clothes at home. More than me, I guess. She leads me into the kitchen without saying anything and she's got the *Herald* spread out on the table. "Hemingway Memorabilia Exchanged for Cat" jumps right out. I read down the article. It re-tells the whole story, including the death of the guard. I look up. Isis is watching me.

"It was an accident," I tell her. "We were only going to take pictures and everything got crazy." I feel like I'm getting a cross-examination from my mother, something I never experienced. The tears run and I pour it all out. I try to tell Isis that we aren't really criminals and would do anything if it was possible to make up for what we'd done, but I'm not very convincing, just pathetic.

Her face is calm and I'm feeling relieved to tell her the truth so I go the whole way with the year limit and how I can't live without Punch. My eyes won't stop flowing. "I'll return Moon-cat when she's better. I promise."

She pulls me to her shoulder and I collapse sobbing. She pats my head for a while until I calm down. "Come upstairs to the circle where I can do a protection spell for you."

"I don't want anything that leaves Punch out," I say.

She shakes her head. "If I help you, it will be good for him too."

I don't believe it can help, but I follow her up. I feel so bad, like the guard being dead is all my fault for going along with the break-in, and everything I'm doing is a big mistake. Isis' knowing the facts puts a whole different feel to it, even without her saying anything.

She takes me to her room, where it's dark with the heavy drapes pulled. She slips off the robe and I see her slim outline. She takes matches to the circle and starts lighting the white candles. I stand there watching the light flicker on her arms until she tells me to slip off my clothes.

I throw my dress on the bed and step out of my panties. The smell of candles and spice and the cool shadowy room are soothing. I smell pine and almost feel I'm naked in a Northern woods, a place where witches have their meetings.

She begins saying words, low, that seem to rhyme. She moves to face me and I close my eyes and stand for her to do what she did the last time, with her fingers hovering over my skin. I smell lavender and feel her rubbing oil on my forehead. I open my eyes.

"Can I touch you intimately, Juliette? I feel so close to you. I want to touch you with love."

I nod. I barely have breath because her voice is so beautiful and I want to feel her soft hands on my skin.

She moves her hands down and strokes my nipples, around and around, smoothing the sweet oil into my skin. She takes more oil and my skin warms and shines in the candle light. I feel the heat through my body. I look at her eyes and they're closed. My nipples are hard into her palms and I'm breathing heavy.

Her hands move down my belly and I've never felt a soft

touch like this. She's smoothing farther downward. I can't move. I don't want to stop her. I feel sweat run down my backbone.

She cups my pubic bone and I feel pressure on my clit. I wait for her fingers to go inside, but they don't. I'm confused. This would be foreplay from a man, but maybe I don't understand a woman – or a witch.

She squats to trail her fingers down my thighs and then massages my feet. I'm shaking with some powerful need. I want more of her touch on my body, warm, soft skin against me, closeness. I'm surrounded by chilly air.

Isis finishes massaging my feet and I'm hot and tingly all through. She repeats Psalm 27 three times and asks the Goddess to grant protection. Still squatting, she turns toward the candles to blow them out one by one. I don't want it to end. I bend and kiss her on the neck. I hunch down next to her and wrap my arms around her back and knees, careful not to scratch her with my splint, and hug her with my face pressed against her shoulder.

I feel her move and I look into her beautiful, bright eyes. She smooths my hair back and kisses me on the lips. She smells so clean and her lips are soft against my mouth, as warm as I could want.

Her body wavers and I take my arms from around her. She stands and clasps my good hand and leads me to the bed. I'm thinking that Punch was expecting this, but I don't care if he knows me better than I do. Having sex with a woman is something I never thought of doing, but now it seems natural, a new experience.

She sits next to me and pulls me into her arms. I nuzzle into her warm chest with my face then snuggle my whole body as close as I can get. My cheek rests on the softest skin I ever felt. She massages the back of my neck and rubs her face in my hair. I close my lips on one of her nipples. I cup her tit and take most of it into my mouth, suck it and let it back out and suck it again, the same way I know it feels good on me. I feel her take a breath of pleasure and her shoulders go back.

I slide down her belly and bury my face in her fine pubic hair. My tongue finds the soft pink inside skin and tiny kernel that moves as I flick it side to side or roll it around. The flavor is salty and sweet like the taste of myself from Punch's lips. I feel her warmth pouring out in her juices and I lick and slurp to get what I can.

I hear her come – a light musical sound, building, then dribbling into a sigh, like nothing I've ever heard. I wait and listen to her breathing, feel her body relax.

"Come up here," she says.

I scoot so we're shoulder to shoulder and she moves part on top of me and kisses my lips again. I'm wondering if she tastes and smells herself on me. She puts her tongue inside and I feel it on mine, delicate, velvety, so different from a man. I play with her mouth at the same time she glides her fingertips down my neck and chest. I should have known everything would be softer, kinder, with a woman. She caresses my skin until I have to stop kissing to get air. She moves on down to taste inside of me with that slender tongue. She makes me come and come. I melt into the feeling. It's like having a man, if I didn't know, but it's different, so comfortable, because we're both the same.

She moves up and I curl against her. She takes me into her arms and my body falls into a foggy dream state. Her cheek touches my forehead and I feel her breathing next to my ear on the pillow. She doesn't let go.

I wake up. I can barely see the outline of her body next to me. I know it's black outside and I need to go home. It could be near morning and I don't want Punch to miss me, even though I'm going to tell him everything.

I touch her shoulder and she moves. Her hand finds my chin and she kisses me. Her breath is clean and sweet, not what I'm used to. I smell myself on her face. I like being next to her.

"Are you leaving?" Isis asks.

"I better."

"Will you come back?"

I don't have an answer. I take a lock of her hair in my fingers, twist it. I can't think.

"Are you okay?"

I nod. "Yeah. I just don't know if I can – because of Punch and everything. Doing it again would be different from once."

"You're right. But one time – so wonderful – means something."

I take a deep breath. "I know." My mind is out of control picturing me with Isis. I see myself having tea, working at the witch shop, Bill and Moon-cat scampering around. It's lunacy. I'm not a lesbian. I never thought of doing anything like that.

She puts her mouth on mine and kisses me again. This time her velvet tongue goes in and I feel chills and heat flaring up. I want to melt into her forever.

I pull away. "I better go now."

She moves aside to let me stand and I find my clothes and sling them on.

"Can we still be friends?" I ask her. "Whatever happens?"

She sits up and takes my hand, the splinted one, pulls me close and whispers – "What do you think? That I only want you for your body?"

"No. I just meant – "

"Don't confuse me with a man, sweet dove."

I want to tell her she's on the wrong track – that Punch and I are special together, but I know I can't explain it. "Punch doesn't want me for my body. He's not so interested in sex. It's more than that."

"Oh? I didn't necessarily mean – "

"I have to go." I take my hand from hers and back up.

"Did you like being with me, Juliette?"

"Yes . . . Yes. I love you." I bolt out of there and down the stairs before she can say anything. I don't know what I'm going to do. I see hazy light from the front window and realize that I better get home fast.

It's dawn when I get there, and Punch is still crashed. He's in his clothes and I can smell alcohol from the doorway, so I'm glad I missed the night's partying. I rinse my face and crawl in next to him for a little more sleep. I put my foot on top of his to feel close. His foot's ice cold.

I sit up and look at his face. It's pale, almost gray. His forehead is cold. I slap his face one side and the other, again and again, many times. There's no response. I find a pulse, put my ear near his mouth and think I feel breath. I try shaking his shoulders and raising his arms. I run to the kitchen and get a piece of ice. I put it on his forehead and run it down his cheeks. It hardly melts. He's like rock. I can't think of anything else. I need help. I run to the phone. He'll say it's stupid – if he wakes up – but I dial 911.

I keep working on him while I wait. Nothing happens. It seems a long time, but once the paramedics get there, they move fast. I tell them about the diabetes and drinking. One guy puts the plastic oxygen cup over Punch's nose and mouth and the other starts an I.V. They strap him down and I hold the screendoor as they wheel him through. I don't know what I'll do if he's in a coma. I can't even think. My head is empty. I'm weighed down with guilt. If I would have been home and not with Isis, maybe I would have been able to do something before it was too late.

I step outside and see the paramedics stop by the pool. One is talking. Then Punch starts yelling. I'm so happy, I fly over there.

"Juliette, what the fuck is going on here? Make these guys let me go."

The paramedic tells me that Punch needs hospital care to be sure he's stable.

"You better go," I tell Punch. "You almost died."

"Juliette, you have to stop doing this." He turns away from me to the paramedic on the other side. "She gets upset and imagines things. I'm fine. I don't have the money to waste on tests and treatments I don't need."

The paramedic shakes his head. "Without the I.V. you might not have woken up."

"This is bullshit," Punch says. "Let me off this thing right now." His eyes bulge and I can see his arms straining at the belt. "Unstrap this bullshit."

"We can't force him to go to the hospital."

I shrug my shoulders. There's no choice.

They won't let him off by the pool. They cart him back into the cottage and unbelt him. He stands up next to the couch and sits right back down. He takes a breath and smooths back his hair. "Thanks for coming out," he says. "Sorry. Juliette panics easily."

I don't say anything. He sends me in the house for the money to pay them. I know he needs to be under a doctor's care, but there's no chance. I feel angry that he won't listen to me. I think of calling Isis to ask her advice, but she might tell me to leave him.

After the paramedics pack up and go, I bring Punch orange juice and some toast. "I'm dead," I say. "I'm going back to bed. If you decide to lie down, call me. I want to keep an eye on you."

"I'm ready to work. Just go on and get some sleep. I'll be fine."

I can tell he's relieved that I'm not up for a discussion. I go in and stretch out, planning to listen to what he's doing out there just in case. I hear him begin to type.

I wake up. Punch is still typing. It's noon. I drag myself into the living room.

"Late night again," he says to me. "Out with the witch?"

"Yeah." I pause. "She gave me a new spell – "

"I'm using her in the book," he says.

"Huh?" I'm surprised he's telling me about it.

"Yeah. It's just the kind of weird detail I need for a novel in Key West – a kooky lesbian chick casting spells."

"Oh. I don't know if you should. She's not kooky."

"That's interesting," he says.

He swivels the chair to look at me. "I'm not going to use her real name. Is that all right with you?"

"I guess." I'm thinking there's only one witch with a witch shop in Key West. I hope he doesn't make her look bad. "She only does good spells, you know?"

"I might need you to help me with some details for a scene. I can't quite picture you two together. I need more depth. I might even like to watch. Would you do that for me?"

I feel my face go red. Normally I'd be flattered that he's asking me to do something important.

"Jul, what's the problem? Huh? Speak up."

The tone of his voice finishes my thinking. "You embarrass me, Punch. I can't do that."

"I bet Isis would oblige. Just ask her."

"I don't know."

"Isn't it part of our deal to go along with each other's ideas? Without question?"

"But I wouldn't ask you to do something like that."

He stares at me. His eyes are cool.

"I'm not even awake yet. Let me go brush my teeth." I head to the bathroom. I hear him go to the computer and I cross to the bedroom. I pull on a sundress and get my towel. "I don't want to disturb you. I'm going to the Shores for a swim. I'll be back if you want to go out to eat."

"Yeah," he says. "Then we can drop over to see Isis."

I kiss him bye and don't say anything. I'm thinking, shit! He should have come with me last night. My head is totally screwed up with worry and loyalties on both sides, and since I didn't tell him what I did, now I'm afraid for him to find out. I don't ever want them to meet.

I stay at the pool as late as I can and worry the whole time. I still can't figure out what I'm going to say to him.

When I get home there's a note. He's gone with Wizard to buy parts for the Triton. I can find him at Tony's later. He's got X's and O's all over the page. Fine. I don't have to deal with any more questions right now.

14

◆◆◆◆◆◆◆◆◆◆◆◆◆◆◆◆

I take a shower, then ride my bike down to Viva's thinking about their mushroom-cheese quesadilla, crab cakes with poblano cream sauce, and my three margaritas. I have to take my mind off Punch and Isis for a little while.

I've finished the food and I'm sipping my third margarita when I see my construction worker friend with the missing tooth. The gap is still open so I guess the epoxy replacement never worked out. He doesn't seem to recognize me, probably too far gone that night to remember anything.

I think about the night I met him and it hits me that it's time to try my flashing routine again. Now that I have my Beretta, maybe I can come up with something interesting to make Punch forget about Isis.

I ride my bike home and put the Beretta and my black wig in a canvas shoulder bag. I don't take any bullets. I pick a dark spot a couple blocks down on Catherine between a tree and a fence. I put the wig on and strip down so I'm ready. I look at the splint. It's not in style for a flasher. When somebody comes, I'll put both hands behind me, the splinted right hand and the left hand with the gun.

There's a fireplug to prop my ass on and I wait with my piece – like I'll call it to Punch – in my lap. I think of some details. It's a warm humid night, so the metal fireplug and cold gun feel good. I picture my sleek silhouette in the dark against the trees. I'm in control with my threatening weapon.

Soon I see a prospect under the next street light. He's tall, middle-aged, muscular, with yellow-blond hair cut short. I think I see the glint of an earring on the left side, the kind of guy that I need a gun to scare. He's walking brisk with his arms crossed, like in deep thought.

It dawns on me that I still haven't planned something clever to say, but I don't want the guy to get away. I step forward, chest out, arms behind my back. I'm about six feet in front of him.

"What the fuck's this?" he says. His voice is gruff. His arms drop to his sides.

"What do you think?" My nerve is suddenly running a little thin.

He laughs and runs his fingers through his hair. "A sex-crazed, teenage hooker?"

My hand goes to my hip. I'm faking guts at this point.

He looks down and crosses his arms. "Rough customer?"

I realize the splint's showing. "No. I'm not a hooker. I'm flashing you."

"Oh . . . great. No raincoat?"

I don't know where to go from here, so I pull out the Beretta. He stiffens a little. "Hey now. What's the deal?"

I have a flash of power, but I'm not sure what to do with it. "Let me see your wallet. Take it out and kick it to me, like in the movies."

He pulls a wallet out, drops it on the ground and kicks it right under the toe of my flip-flop. When I bend to reach for it, there's a rush of air, a push. That fast I'm doubled under his body, the air squeezed out of me. In another second he has the gun wrenched from my hand and my arm twisted behind me. He pulls my arm to straighten me up.

"Fuck. Get off me! I wasn't going to steal anything. It's not loaded."

He unbends my arm and turns me to face him, holding my wrist. I see the Beretta stuck in his waist band. He looks into my eyes and down my body, past my fear-stiffened nipples. He points to the gun. "What were you planning to do with this little thing?"

"Just scare you."

"Are you on something?"

"Margaritas. Is there a law against that?"

He shakes his head. "Not if you're old enough. There are laws against disorderly conduct and armed robbery."

"I wasn't going to take your money. Just going to look at your I.D. See who I was flashing . . . where you're from."

"Take a look." He opens the wallet close to my face and I see an I.D. of some kind. It says Det. Albert Woodly. I take a big breath. "Detective?"

"Uh huh. Actually this is from the state of New York. I start with the Key West Police next week. I moved down here to get away from all the craziness." He shakes his head. "Then I run into you."

"You're not going to arrest me, are you? Take me to jail naked? Drag me in for everybody to gawk at and lock me in a freezing cold cell?"

He shakes his head again, like he doesn't believe what he's hearing.

Guess I'm not dazzling him with bullshit. "Flashing doesn't hurt anybody," I say. "I was just doing it for something exciting – for a book."

His eyes flick down my body. "Exposing yourself and holding someone at gunpoint? What kind of book?"

"Not my book, somebody else's, a great writer."

"Is everybody in Key West a writer? I'm working on a screen-play myself. Look, young lady, pointing a gun at somebody is assault. It's a felony."

"It's not loaded. Does that count?"

He's looking around. "Where are your clothes?"

I point to my dress hanging on a branch. He takes my arm and walks me over. "You're not going to run, are you? I'll catch you before you get three steps."

"No."

He lets go and I sling on my dress and step into my thong. He's watching me the whole time.

"What is it you want? Attention?"

"No, I don't want anything – I don't know what I want. I'm doing this to see what happens – like I said – for a book. I know it's stupid."

"What about the gun? Is it yours?"

"It's mine. I bought it at Uncle Sam's – for protection."

"Yeah? If you had any sense, you wouldn't need so much protection." He pulls it out and pops open the chamber, then ejects the clip. "This is not only a felony, it's a dangerous game you're playing. Ever think about getting raped, beaten, and murdered?"

"It's Key West."

"Don't fool yourself. Not every guy on the street's as nice as I am." He points to the splint. "What happened there?"

"Accident."

He stands looking at the gun and then at me. He shakes his head. "I should take you in. In fact, I'm really stretching my conscience by not doing it. But I'm going to escort you on home. This is your lucky night."

Isis comes to mind – the spell? I pick up my bag and slip on my flip-flops. I'm ready to get moving before he changes his mind. I point ahead and we walk the short distance and turn onto Watson.

I'm hoping Punch isn't up. With him at this time of night, things could get real complicated. This isn't the kind of interesting story I had in mind.

I pull out my key and unlock the gate and Woodly follows me to the door. I see the light's off inside, which means Punch probably isn't home yet.

"I'd like to see your driver's license and the receipt for the gun, if you don't mind."

He waits on the porch and I go inside to find them. When I step back out, I see Punch in the dark walking toward the steps.

He stops, sways. "Who the fuck are you?"

"Detective Al Woodly. Who are you?"

"Fuck. Punch Evans. I live here."

"I'm bringing your daughter home. She's been out on the street pointing a gun."

Punch is showing mass confusion. His brain isn't working too well. "She's not – she was what?"

"It's okay. The policeman just walked me home." I hand over my license to Woodly. He studies it, but doesn't say anything about my last name being Halliburton, instead of Evans, like Punch's daughter would be. Our complexion differences must not be that obvious in the dark either. He takes the receipt, looks, and hands the stuff back.

"I don't think it's safe for Juliette here to be toting a gun around dark alleys in the middle of the night," he says.

Punch steps up on the porch next to me where there's light from the window. He's holding the wall to keep steady. "You took the gun?"

"I'll tell you about it in the morning. Go get your contacts out. I'll be right in."

He frowns, then slowly and carefully opens the screendoor and goes inside.

"I can see it's not worth giving him the details, but you'd better listen to me. I'm stretching the limit this time. If I catch you hanging around in the dark or hear anything about a naked woman, you're going to get hauled in and charged with everything there is. Clear?"

"Yes, sir. Can I have the gun back?"

"I'd like to keep it from you." He hands it over slowly, butt end toward me, muzzle down. "You're more likely to get hurt using this than protecting yourself."

"Thank you, officer."

"I'm trying to help you, you understand? Maybe you need psychological counseling. I should have taken you in."

"It's Key West, right? Full of happy bohemians. Not like New York City."

"Yeah. Let's keep it that way. I mean it – I'm on the lookout for you."

He leaves and I go inside. I'm rattled. I look into the bedroom. Punch is zonked. I wonder if he'll remember this in the morning. I'm getting a huge backlog of things to explain, that I'm afraid to. I don't want to have secrets from Punch. I feel like I'm growing away from him. All I wanted was a wild story, and I manage to get a cop keeping an eye on me.

I wake up before Punch and start cooking his favorite breakfast, biscuits and gravy, eggs and sausage. I'm tired of country cooking myself. I used to have to choke down too much of it. Punch comes walking out slowly.

"What the fuck was that all about last night?"

I hand him a plate of biscuits sopping in peppery gravy with an egg and sausage on the side. "Didn't work out. It was one of my ideas, wild stuff for the book – I got caught by a cop."

"Lucky he didn't take you in. They would have fingerprinted you."

I swallow a breath. "He said I was lucky not to be raped and murdered."

"That's a cop for you."

I open a biscuit on the plate in front of me and steam comes up. I ladle on some thick white gravy and think how homey it would feel if we weren't living such crazy lives – and if we didn't need to die soon. I don't know why I'm even thinking about it – I hate homeyness.

"I wonder, Punch – Key West being so small – would the cop know about the size of the clothes left in Hemingway's bedroom? He might think about me exposing myself and connect it."

"I bet he's thinking about you naked all right."

"Punch, I'm serious."

"I doubt it – there are lots of scrawny women around this town. No sense worrying. He would have taken you in already."

"I'm not so sure. Scrawny?"

He shrugs. "Slender. Petite."

"I'm going to stay off the streets as much as I can at night – and carry a flashlight, so I'm not breaking any law on my bicycle. Maybe he'll forget all about me."

"I doubt that," Punch says.

We finish breakfast and Punch doesn't say anything about Isis. He goes right to the computer. I can hear serious typing going on while I'm doing the dishes. Poor as my plan turned out, he's got something to write.

That afternoon I go over to the witch shop. Since Isis already knows about the Hemingway deal, I want to tell her about the cop, get her feeling on it. I wonder how I can relate the story without admitting I was naked.

I walk in and she's helping a customer. There are three people in the store, pretty good for off-season. When they leave she comes to me smiling and takes me into her arms for a soft kiss. "I was just thinking about you," she says.

I hug her back. I wonder if she was thinking of sex.

"Come have some tea. You look jittery."

I tell her about Woodly almost arresting me, but I skip the nudity. I say I got scared in the dark and pulled out the Beretta. I can see worry on her face, although she tells me the protection is working. "But you can't rely on witchcraft to save you if you're out looking for trouble. You shouldn't be walking down Catherine – or any dark street – that late at night. Much less carrying a gun."

"I know. I'm an idiot."

She smooths my hair. "Come back this evening when I close. We'll do a spell for both of you. Bring me a picture of Punch. Remember, you have a good witch on your side."

I sigh. "I don't know if I can sleep with you again."

"You mean make love?"

I make myself say it. "Make love. I don't know."

"It's all up to you. You made the move last time, remember?"

"Yes."

"I love you, Juliette – for your beauty and your perseverance and sweetness in trying to help Punch. You have no idea of your potential. With a little guidance in the right direction, you have your whole life to soar and reach for the moon. Use your wings."

My head has tilted toward the floor. She lifts my chin and I feel her eyes penetrate me. I feel a tingle move through my chest into my spine. It's a strange sensation. Suddenly I believe fully in her power.

"I was tempted to put a love spell on you when we first met. I considered snipping a pinch of your hair that first night while you slept, but I knew it would be wrong. I hesitate to interfere with karma, no matter how sure I am of the good. You love me in your own way. I'll leave everything up to you and the Goddess."

I twitch under her stare. I never thought about her having the ability to affect my feelings.

"Don't worry – you have your own power. I can only help you along. You have to use the magic inside yourself, set your priorities. You can't base your life on what you think other people want you to do."

I know she's talking about Punch and his influence over me,

but I can't think only of myself. She doesn't understand my priorities, and I can't explain. "I'll try to come back later," I tell her.

Punch cooks dinner that night because he says we need to save money. He's tired of gourmet food anyway. He makes chicken and mashed potatoes and black-eyed peas. It's good, but using the stove heats the cottage up so much I lose my appetite. Punch never has one anyway. I know we're eating at home because of the Triton expenses, but I hold back my remarks. Punch has gone to a lot of trouble to cook. He says the credit cards should be here in a few days and we can eat out.

He goes off to Tony's, where he has a running tab, and I get in the pool to cool off. I want to put my head under and really swim, so I decide I've had the fucking splint on my hand long enough. I sit on the lounge chair and unwrap all the gauze. The pain's been gone a long time and it's not like I need it perfect. Fuck. It's probably only got to last me a few months. When I swim it feels a little weak against the water, but it's fine.

I go inside and turn on the TV to watch a cooking show with Bill. I get him his stuffed bear and roll a joint. I'm not ready to visit Isis. I don't know what to say or do. I let Bill go at the bear three times and then he falls asleep right in the middle of the floor. It's so easy for him to have a wild time at any moment. I don't know what Punch and I are going to do. I'm worried about his progress on the book.

15

◆◆◆◆◆◆◆◆◆◆◆◆◆◆◆◆◆◆◆

In a few days Punch opens the mail and tells me that all the credit cards he's applied for have been denied. "They say I've exceeded my credit limit."

I'm ready to cry. "Fuck! What about selling the Triton?"

I see his color deepen. He's on edge. He hasn't let me see my bank statement this month. "It's not ready. I don't want to talk about that. It's not an option right now."

"Fucking great," I say. "I don't know how to have fun anymore, Punch. We're never together. Now we can't go out to eat or do anything. I'm going crazy roasting to death in this place. I won't last till fucking October."

I expect him to get mad back at me, but I don't even care.

Instead, he pulls me onto his lap on the couch. "I'm thinking I'll put an ad in the paper to sell the car."

Immediately my eyes start overflowing. I don't want to sell the car. It's true we can walk to Fausto's for groceries, and most days we don't even start the engine, but it was Pop's car, and as much as I hated that man, I guess I still love him.

Then I remember Punch sold his own car to add to our starter money. I feel selfish. I wipe my eyes. "Sell it," I say, but the sobs start and then the heaves. I have to run into the bathroom.

I finally quiet my stomach down and Punch comes in. "We're not going to sell the car. I know how you feel about it. I'll think of something else." He puts the toilet lid down, sits, and motions me to his lap. He plays with my hair and I start to feel better. He takes my hand and walks me into the bedroom, kisses me. At first I'm stiff, feeling mad at him and guilty about Isis. I want to get away from his eyes so I go through the motions, pulling off his pants and taking him into my mouth. I think of her, the softness, the feeling of her tongue. I wonder if I'm doing anything different, if he'll be able to tell that something's changed. But he sighs and motions me to change positions so he can get his mouth into my pussy. I relax, and sweat, and listen to the rushes roll through me, feel the tingles. I'm myself again. It's all I want, skin-on-skin with Punch.

Afterward he tells me he's going to the liquor store and he'll stop for a video. He wants to spend the whole night with me. I hug him hard.

In a short time, he comes back excited. "I've got *Bonnie and Clyde,*" he tells me. "You're going to love this."

We settle down like a regular couple, sweating together on the couch, with Bill in my lap. The film has a sexy, fast-moving beginning. I can relate to Bonnie taking off with Clyde. She's got nothing in that town and never will have. They're choosing to live for the moment, just like me and Punch.

Punch nudges me when Bonnie poses by the car with her machine gun. "There you are, Juliette, with your gun. Only you're prettier."

I smile and kiss him for what he means as a compliment, but I know I'm not as tough as Bonnie, and I hope not as desperate. I don't want to shoot anyone.

The story starts to get depressing, more bad times than good, fights between them. Then the funny part – Bonnie writes their story for the newspaper. "Punch, did you get your idea from this?" I ask him.

Punch shakes his head. "I forgot all about it. I'm not writing a crime novel. This is our story, babycakes, of two people trying to survive the motherfucking, isolating, money-grubbing, psychotic, cocksucking, modern world."

I snort. "Oh, sorry I asked."

"It's truth, m' dear. The only thing worth writing about."

At the end of the movie, I cover my eyes. I know what's coming. But I open them too soon, not figuring on slow motion. There's Bonnie, her pretty dress a bloody rag of bullet holes as she rolls halfway out the car door.

I put my head on Punch's chest and shiver despite the sweat. "I'm glad you're not writing a crime book. I don't want to end up like that."

He shrugs. "What's the difference? It's over fast. They went down together, m' dear. Better to die in a hail of bullets – do not go gentle into that good night."

I kiss his soft neck. "Gentle's good sometimes." Isis pops into my head. I think of how pure and orderly her life is. I squeeze my face into Punch's neck again, squeeze Isis out. The time to die is starting to feel real close.

I watch TV and Punch sips his rum until he dozes off. I don't wake him to take out his contacts. I sit there holding his thigh even though there's a coating of sweat between us. I don't want to fall asleep and have nightmares. He nudges me at dawn, when I've finally dozed off in the coolness, and I follow him into the bedroom.

The next day at breakfast I tell him to go ahead and sell the car. "We might as well enjoy the money. It's selfish of me to hold onto something we don't need – just for sentimental reasons."

"No. That's settled. I have another idea. One that's interesting and will save money at the same time."

He won't tell me anything except not to plan on cooking

dinner. We'll be eating late. He goes off by himself for a couple hours and returns with grocery bags, which he puts into the closet and tells me not to open.

I swim and hang out all day, feeling anxious, while he writes. I'm starved by nine when he finally says it's time to go eat.

He throws me one of the bags from the closet. "Here's your stuff. Take a look."

I pull out a short dark wig and some purple cotton pants and a matching top. The top is big with flowing sleeves and multi-colored, sequined butterflies, something a heavier, older woman might wear. There's a pair of jeans in the bag too, right size.

"Goodwill had a sale on purple," Punch says. He shows me a lavender guayabera shirt and a felt hat and mask he has for himself.

I hold my blouse to my shoulders. It hangs halfway to my knees. "I don't want this, Punch. It's ugly."

"The idea is for nobody to recognize you."

"We're taking Bill?"

"No. Oh, these are yours too." He throws me a fancy feather mask, the kind that covers the eyes and nose, and a pair of gloves. "No Bill tonight. We'll bring him a doggy bag."

I can't figure it, but I pull the shirt over my head.

"Take that back off," Punch says. "We put these on when we get there. Wear the jeans and a dark T-shirt. Pin up your hair so it'll fit under the wig."

"You're making me nervous, Punch."

"Where's the gun?"

Now I'm getting upset. "Punch, I can't take that gun out again. Look what happened the last time."

"Nothing."

"Something."

"I'm the one who's going to carry it," he says, "so don't worry." He goes into the bedroom and I hear him open a drawer.

"Nightstand," I call. I know there's no choice in the long run.

He brings the Beretta out and pops open the chamber, slides out the clip. It looks like a toy for sure in his big hand. "Empty."

"Uh huh. You're not thinking of loading it, are you?"

"I don't know. I might need to scare somebody."

"Uh uh. I won't go. I mean it, Punch." My voice starts to crack, thinking how I'm cutting myself off from him, feeling out of control. "I mean it."

He looks at me. "Aren't we together? We're supposed to be together in all of this."

"Please, Punch. It's too dangerous. I don't want to kill anybody – else."

He puts the gun in one of the big pockets of his shirt, rolls it up, and stashes it in the bag. "Okay. You win. Get dressed and let's go. We want to get there before the kitchen closes. We're going to Louie's Backyard."

"Dressed in this?"

He nods and walks into the bathroom.

I know this isn't going to be a peaceful meal at Louie's, but I'm starting to salivate while I put on my jeans. I trust Punch. He must have something set up with one of the chefs.

I've always wanted to eat at Louie's, in the back under the trees, next to dog beach, with waves rolling in right up to the deck. We've only had drinks at their Afterdeck Bar because the restaurant is so expensive. Out at the bar they have cute signs saying "No unescorted dogs allowed," but dogs still wander through from their beach. It's a beach no wider than a driveway, but the only one in Key West for four-leggers. I'm thinking we can escort Bill for dinner on our last night and spend every cent we have left. I feel self-pity tears starting, but will them away, let them dry without blinking. There's still a chance for us.

Punch says he wants to ride bicycles. I'm amazed the way he can stay sober enough when he's got mischief in mind. It's about a ten-minute ride. I'm trying to remember if the time's up on the protection spell. We walk the bikes down the side of the building

under the trees past the bike stands, and shove the bikes into the
bushes. Punch says he already checked out the way to the kitchen.

"What are we doing?" I ask him.

"We're going to see the chef personally. One of the best in
town. I'll order whatever he recommends."

"I hope we're not going to steal." Pop always said that taking
food isn't a crime if you're hungry. But gourmet food? It's true
that I am really, really hungry by now. I just wish Punch wasn't
holding the gun. "Couldn't you fake it, Punch. Put your finger in
your pocket and pretend?"

He looks at me. "Why do that when I have a gun? Come on,
where's my Jul? Get wild."

Yeah, I think, I'm forgetting the point, to be wild in Key
West, while the going's good. Nobody gets hurt. Fuck with the
world like it fucks with us.

We huddle behind the bushes and slip on our disguises. Punch
pulls out a black half-mask for himself and I put on mine. There's
no good or bad, I tell myself, just interesting or boring.

"Walk this way," he says. I giggle and he looks back and
hunches over, then puts his finger to his lips. Nobody can say
that line without doing an Igor imitation, no matter what.

I follow him around the dumpster and up the wood stairs.
He pauses outside the door. "Okay, this is the kitchen. Stay behind
me. Don't talk."

He opens the door and I hear people up ahead, utensil noises
and sizzling. I smell garlic. Punch motions for me to wait. He
takes out the Beretta and peeks around the corner. He waves me
to follow. It dawns on me that, if this is real, I am committing
armed robbery. It's too late to stop – unless I leave Punch right
now. I can't.

We take a small step inside. It's part of the kitchen, filled with
stainless steel equipment. Steam is rising from the stove where a
guy in a chef hat is sideways to us turning shrimp on a grill. A
strawberry blond guy with a beard, wearing a baseball cap, is

dribbling butter into a sauce pan. Across the worktable that runs
the length of the room, a big guy is bent over two plates of food,
wiping drips off the edges. He's reading out loud at the same time
– "Salmon, black shrimp two times, a hair straight up – "

He glimpses Punch to the side with the gun, drops his towel.
"Christ."

The others look up and put down what they're doing. "Hey,
that's not funny," the griller yells.

"Si, señor. Is fonny," Punch says. He's using a fake accent,
trying to sound Cuban, I guess. "Especiales, por favor. Deenner
for two y chocolata dessert. Is best restaurant in Cayo Hueso,
no?"

I'm watching amazed, but I'm scared that somebody else
might come in behind us. Punch whispers to me, "Let's move to
the other side, so I can cover both doors."

We walk slowly and carefully sideways past the chefs. I can
feel the heat building as we get closer to the stoves. Punch points
the gun at the guy with the chef's hat. We step close to him to
pass a giant mixer on the floor.

"Whoa! Don't shoot," the guy yells.

"I'm in charge here," says the guy with the plates. "Okay. No
problem. We have plenty of the special tonight. I have two all
ready to go." He sweeps his open hand over the two plates of
delicately browned square fillets of fish in the middle of a light
orange sauce. Asparagus and pink shrimp peek from under the
fish. He sprinkles on some chopped spring onions just like on TV
and nestles a slice of orange, sprig of dill, and a tiny orchid next
to the fish. Even with all the fear my mouth starts to water.

"Voilà?"

"Más," Punch mutters. "Cuatro – Need four of thees," he
says to the chef.

"Okay. Okay, but it's going to take a few minutes – uno
momento. You're lucky this is off-season on a weeknight, amigo."
He gives orders to the other two, and they all get busy. They're

crossing over each other and don't seem to be doing their regular jobs, so I guess he's trying to hurry everything up. I'm as antsy as they are. I'm thinking two meals would have been plenty – Punch won't even finish one – but I don't say anything. He's getting all this to make sure I have enough. By now sweat is running inside all my clothes and my chin is dripping.

"I have to go to the walk-in for the chocolate nirvana," the chef says. He points, "Desserts are in there."

Punch looks toward the walk-in. He whispers to me, "I don't want him going in there. If you want dessert, you have to get it yourself."

I think of the cool air and that I might find a creme brûlée, but there's no way I'm going to cut myself off from Punch. I shake my head.

"No chocolata," Punch tells them.

Just then a waitress comes around the corner. "What's holding up my fish?" She sees Punch with the gun. "Oh, take your time. No fucking hurry – fuck my tip! I better get back to my tables – "

Punch swings the gun toward her. "Back, gringa."

She halts. "Sure, bandido," she says. She crosses in front of us, holding the edge of the long worktable as she walks. She's a tall, shapely blond in a short skirt, looks a little like Cindy Crawford. I look at Punch to see if he notices. He's all business.

"It's okay, Tina," says the chef. "We're making them carry-outs."

The guys are all moving fast, throwing ingredients into the pans, grilling, and saucing, with fire licking close to their fingers. Sweat beads on their faces. I don't have a good view like on the Food Channel, but I see shrimp, fish, and portobello mushrooms searing on the grill and smell the delicious odors. One chef flips asparagus and it hops a foot above the pan and lands back in.

There are lots of big knives in reach – good thing we have the gun. The two guys get our food together and hand over the finished plates to the boss chef. He slides the portions into square styrofoam containers and adds the garnishes. "It's not going to look or taste as good by the time you get it home," he says. He looks at the Beretta. "But I guess you have to eat and run – run and eat, I mean."

We chuckle to make him feel good. I'm trying not to slip over the edge of laughter into hysterics. Finally the dinners are all together, and Punch hands the two large plastic bags to me.

"Gracias," Punch says to the chefs and bows his head.

"My pleasure," says the chef. His eyebrows are up, like he still thinks we're crazy, but he sounds relaxed now, even amused. "You're right." He points to himself. "I'm the best chef in Key West. Bon appétit."

We back out of there and then turn and run. I have a wild urge to laugh, but I keep my mouth shut and move as fast as I can. We step outside into the bushes and strip off our disguises and stuff them back into the bags we left there. I feel the cool breeze on my sweaty skin and take a breath of sea air. I can smell the peppery sweet aroma coming from our carry-outs.

I put the plastic containers in the bags with our costumes and set them gently in the bike baskets. Punch looks around. There's no commotion so we ride fast up to the street and take a right toward home. As soon as we're out of sight I let the laughs fly. The relief is heaven. Nobody seems to be following us. No sirens. We zoom and we laugh. We laugh so hard I have to stop so I don't crash into parked cars. Punch makes a U-turn and comes up next to me. We hug each other across our bikes. I'm crying and my jaws ache from the strain. Finally we pull ourselves together to ride.

When we get home Punch tells me that his extra meal is for Bill. I kiss him. "You're such a sweetheart."

"Claro, mi gringita," he says.

"When did you learn Spanish?"

"I only know a few words. I thought it would be a good idea, in case they tried to identify us. I need to look up some more."

I feed Bill his fish and he eats it so fast I know he doesn't care about the freshness and delicate taste, or the perfect texture of the asparagus. Punch is eating his like a robot in front of the TV. I sit down and appreciate every bite of mine.

The next morning we check the paper. Punch is disappointed when there's no coverage.

"I guess they didn't bother to call the police on us," I say. "Or it was too late to get the story in."

"Maybe the chef was flattered and didn't want us to get caught. Chefs can be real prima donnas. Boost their egos and it goes a long way."

"Like writers?"

He looks at me.

I laugh. "Not you. I'm just kidding. You don't even show anything to anybody."

"I did show somebody – a couple weeks ago."

"You did?" I feel my stomach drop. I'm hurt he'd show somebody else and not me. "Who?"

"Our neighbor – Albin."

"What did he think?"

"He told me I had interesting character development, but I need to strengthen the plot. He says it's too episodic."

"Episodic?"

"Incidents without direct cause and effect connection. It *is* episodic. That's the style. I've been partly modeling it on *Candide* – the classic, by Voltaire. I'll tie everything up in the end. I have some rewriting to do."

"Did he like it?"

"He wasn't overwhelmed."

"Maybe he just has different taste. When can I read the novel, Punch?"

He gets up from the table to wash his plate. "Not yet. I told you, I don't want you to see it till it's finished."

"What if I don't have time? I'll be dead."

"You won't be dead."

"It's my baby too."

He steps toward the door. "Okay. Time for me to go cultivate our garden, m' dear."

"Huh?"

" – a line from Voltaire. I mean I better get back to work. In this cruel world, Juliette, darlin', we have to keep on plugging to make life bearable." He stops and turns back to me. "Until the end of October."

I nod. "I'm with you – to live and die – no matter if you try to stop me."

He goes to the computer.

I feel paralyzed. We couldn't have the same kind of freedom if we were living normal lives, and I don't want to watch Punch get sick and die, but our time is too short. There won't be time to sell the book, even if he gets it finished, and that's what I'm counting on to turn his life around.

I go into the bedroom and fall back into bed with my face in the pillow. I feel Bill nuzzling my neck. I sit up and pet him. I'm not going to waste time feeling gloomy. I need to keep doing what I can. I take the sheet and wipe my eyes. It's time to find a photo and take it to Isis, get some more magic.

Isis lets me in and gives me a kiss on the forehead. I feel guilty knowing I'm there to save Punch, and all the while Isis wants to be my lover. I admire her ability to let the universe take its course when she might have the power to make things go her way.

I tell her I'm sorry it took me so long to come back, that everything has gotten crazy.

I follow her upstairs and she sets up the white candles in a circle and lights them. She slips off her robe and motions to me. "The spell will have more power with your love behind it. It will help you both."

I hand her the picture of Punch. It's a silly one of him in his

Neptune costume, with trident and seashell crown, from our first Fantasy Fest, but it's all I could find.

She looks at it and chuckles. "So we're asking the Goddess to protect a god? All right. It'll work."

"He's a god to me."

"I know. He's lucky." She puts the picture at the top of the circle and we kneel facing it.

This time she doesn't touch me or do anything toward my body, just concentrates on Punch. I know she's being careful to respect my wishes. I repeat the prayers with her. "Under grace and for the good of all may the Goddess grant protection for Punch, here pictured, and Juliette, this pure dove," she says.

I'm ashamed when I hear those words because I haven't told her about the robbery and I'm no longer sure our being protected is for the good of all. I think I've just made her waste her time.

On the way home I make the turn onto Duval and there's a police car parked ahead of me. I want to turn around but it's too late. Al Woodly is standing next to the car and he motions to me. I take the surprised look off my face, but it's probably too late. I put on the brakes and squeak to a stop next to him.

"I see you had your splint taken off," he says.

"All cured."

"I hope you're taking better care of yourself now. Staying out of trouble?"

"Yes."

He's looking me over.

I hold the bike between my legs and put my arms out, sort of showing him I'm wearing clothes and not packing a weapon. I'm trying hard to look normal. I'm blushing, but in the bright sun, maybe he can't tell.

"I wondered about you. I almost stopped by to take you out for lunch, but I thought your friend probably wouldn't let you."

"Punch is my boyfriend, and I just don't date other people."

"I figured that out. I just wanted to talk to you. You're a nice girl and need to learn a few things – like who to avoid in Key West."

"I have Punch to watch out for me."

"He wasn't on duty when I found you roaming around naked, was he?"

I purse my lips and put one foot up on a pedal.

"Wait," he says. He hands me a card with his name and the number at the police station. "In case you change your mind about lunch. You know what a nice guy I am."

"Thanks," I say. I give a push and head across the street. I wonder if he's watching my dress blow up around my hips. He seems sincere, but maybe he's just looking for evidence to arrest me.

16

◆◆◆◆◆◆◆◆◆◆◆◆◆◆◆◆◆

Punch is ready to hit another place already that night.
I'm thinking, on one hand, this is good for him. He's not going
to get roaring drunk for forty-eight hours in a row, a new record.
On the other hand, it's a lot of risk. My nerves can't take this
every fucking night.

I don't say anything and put on my jeans. We hop on the
bikes with our brown bags on the handlebars and breeze down
Catherine.

Punch is leading and he hollers back to me. "Monty knows
all the restaurants inside and out, and he loves to talk."

"He's helpful all right."

"All we need is a driver – could use a getaway car." He laughs.
"Maybe Isis – a getaway broom!"

"Is fonny," I yell. "Better choice than Wizard with the Triton!"

I want to bite my tongue as soon as I say it, but he doesn't
answer. At least I shut him up about Isis.

We cruise down Simonton and he makes a left on Angela. We
zoom past the witch shop and I see Punch looking. Now he
knows where it is. I hope Isis doesn't see us go by.

"Italian tonight," Punch calls. He turns down an alley and

we come to the back entrance of Antonia's. The Copa is being rebuilt next door where it burned down, and we park the bikes between some piles of block, where it's dark enough nobody will spot them. We put on our disguises and Punch lugs a big bag of cement mix and sets it near the back door of the restaurant.

"It's an easy job," he says, "kitchen right off here, isolated except for one double-door from the dining room."

He pulls the gun out and tries the knob. It turns. He winks at me and opens the door a crack. I step in behind him, gritting my teeth to stay calm, careful not to make a noise.

The kitchen set-up is another solid room of shining stainless steel and steaming heat. The four chefs are all busy with their heads down, working hard. I wonder if they ever get to eat.

Punch motions with the gun. "Thees eez steek up," he yells. "Two orders garlic rolls, salata, fettucine alfredo – pronto."

The chefs are staring. "Alfredo's not on our menu," one says. "Why not try the fettucine All'Antonia? Mushrooms and peas with a magnificent cream sauce."

"I wish you would have asked me first," I whisper to Punch. "If you told me ahead, I could've studied a menu." I turn to the chefs. "Bueno, muy bueno. Y sopa y uno tiramisù y uno cannoli," I add. "Por favor."

Punch looks at me, then waves the gun. "Vámonos!"

They start moving fast, boiling pasta, swirling cream into mushrooms, and setting up the plates. This time the walk-in is handy and a chef brings out our desserts. "Carry-out," Punch instructs them.

He reaches out to take the bags and I'm thinking how easy this has been. There's a rush to Punch's left. Somebody plows into him. The guy grabs for the gun, but Punch dodges and hits him with his shoulder. The guy goes down and Punch holds the gun on him. "No move, gringo. No move."

"Nick, don't be crazy. You okay?" another guy yells. I'm shaking. Punch is holding the Beretta steady.

Nick turns. He sits up and straightens his chef shirt. "I won't move. Just get outta here. Shouldn't mess with Italians," he says.

The main chef hands over the bags. "I know you'll enjoy the fettucine," he says. "Best in Key West."

I pull on Punch's shirt and we back out. Punch slings the bag of cement in front of the door and smiles. We sprint to the bikes and rip up the next block. I come alongside Punch. He grins at me. "Good job ordering the dessert."

"I was scared, Punch. That was close. What if that guy decided to fight you? Think he's in the mafia?"

"Macho crap. Wouldn't have fought. I had the gun."

"He could've been a looney and called your bluff. You never know."

"No bluff."

The way he says it, I know instantly what he means. I've been stupid to think he didn't load up.

"Look. If you carry a gun, you have to be able to shoot it. But see, I didn't. I'm sorry I couldn't tell you before. You're too naive about things."

I'm glaring at him. I can't even speak.

"I wouldn't shoot to kill. It's only for emergencies, in case somebody goes for a weapon."

I'm visualizing what could've happened, a ripped-up leg, a shoulder. I imagine blood splashing over stainless steel, the searing pain of a bullet. It's my fault. I bought the motherfucking gun. I don't know where my fucking mind was.

17

◆◆◆◆◆◆◆◆◆◆◆◆◆◆◆◆

The next morning I walk into the living room where Punch is reading the paper.

"They got us this time," he says. "An unidentified Latin couple held up Antonia's for fettucine All'Antonia, stracciatelli soup, tiramisù, and cappucinos to go at ten o'clock last night. The couple wore masks and took only food, holding the kitchen crew at gunpoint until they finished preparation."

"Almost got it right. I can't believe they bought our accents."

"This is great. We're set." He reads, "Chef Nick Granti made an unsuccessful attempt to knock the gun from the man's hand. 'It was crazy,' the chef later stated. 'I risked my life over a couple dinners – not worth it, even though the food here is the best on the island.'

"Let that be a lesson to the rest of them," Punch says.

"Punch," I tell him. "I want to sell the car. We can't hold up a restaurant every night."

He raises his eyebrows at me. "Juliette, this is the best idea I've had so far. It's great. I was thinking three times a week. We can cook at home three nights and take Bill out and pay the other night. Babycakes, we're going to be famous."

"I don't know."

"Look, they're enjoying the publicity. I haven't felt better or had more fun in years."

"You're feeling good?"

"Drinking less, that's for sure."

He knows what I want to hear. "How many restaurants have kitchens we can sneak into?"

"Plenty."

"I don't know, Punch."

"That's interesting. Something's changed – in your attitude. You never objected to my ideas before, not like this."

"Let's just sell the car so we don't have so much pressure. We can do what we want, not have to hurt anybody."

"You already expressed your feelings about the car – it's extremely important to you. Now when I have a solution to everything, all of a sudden you change your mind."

I can see how strong he is on this and it does stop him from drinking. I'm sure it's good inspiration for the book, and will be good publicity if we ever get that far.

"Are you changing your mind about being with me? You can, you know. I told you I don't expect you to follow me to the grave."

"No, Punch. Don't even say it." I pull his face down to me and smash my cheek hard against his. "It makes me feel bad when you say that – like you don't think I love you. It's just the gun that scares me – I swear. I want to take it back to Uncle Sam's before somebody gets hurt."

"No, Jul. We need the gun to get their attention, put some drama into it. There's no other way."

I know I've lost the argument, but I'm determined. "I'm only trying to make sense."

"Just stop, Juliette. You'll do what you want, just like every-body else."

He's getting his wallet and I know he's ready to bolt, and I won't see him for the rest of the day. I'll be walking around the house like a zombie while he sits with the guys in Tony's all afternoon making himself sick, and he won't do any writing. I throw on a dress from the chair, grab my purse, and step in front of him. "You stay here and work on your book. I'll leave you alone."

I run out down the sidewalk and through the gate without looking back. I don't know where I'm going. I can't go to Isis and impose myself more on her good will. I get in the car and drive to Higgs Beach.

It's deserted. I sit with the windows open and watch the seagulls. They're laughing like maniacs. It's a sound I love when things are okay, but they're mocking me right now. I'm sweating buckets, but my insides are cold. The gagging starts and I open the door to get sick, but nothing comes up, just spit. Not even much of that.

I don't last long with myself. I know Punch is right. The restaurants are having a chuckle over us. The newspaper has something to write about, and Punch isn't going to shoot anybody. He wouldn't do that. He should shoot somebody like me who needs shooting.

I pull a joint out of my purse and light it, take a long hit. I know he can't stay straight enough to do a robbery three times a week anyway. I'm already amazed he's done it twice. But that shows there's hope for him, that he can stay off the booze when he wants to. Okay, that's a fantasy. I take another good hit and put the joint out. When the newness wears off, Punch will be in Tony's every night and that will be the end of it. So what am I worrying about? I start the car. We don't have much time left and I'm going to be with Punch and use it all – use it up the wild way we set out to, without all the fucking worrying and cry-babying.

As I'm walking toward the cottage, I see that the door's shut.

Punch is already gone. I should have known he couldn't work while we were in a fight. He can only drink when that happens.

I turn on the Food Channel and try to watch, but I can't pay much attention. Life's a shit. It's all fucked. Hog's snorting up truffles. Fuck him. Fat chef stuffing a duck. Everything is shit. Lavender-peach torte. I can't even work up a drool. I turn it off, get a half glass of rum, gulp most of it down, and go into the bedroom. I can't do anything. I ruin everything. I just decided I wasn't going to cry-baby anymore and now I'm going to and I don't give a piss-fuck. I'm going to do whatever Punch wants. Without him, I don't have any reason to live or breathe.

I jump up out of bed with my nose streaming and eyes running so hard I can barely see. I take my rum and stumble into the kitchen, banging against the table as I pass by. I pick up a knife from the sink. It's a serrated one and has chocolate dried on it from where Punch sliced off a bite of tiramisù. I put it to my wrist and I'm thinking I can die right now and Punch will see how much I love him. But I'm not ready to die. I want him to be there watching when I do it. I want him to realize how far I'll go for him – and stop me.

I take the knife to my thigh and brace myself. I'll show him how serious I am. I draw crosswise – don't even feel it. The scalloped edge disappears inside the cut and the blood runs down. I move the knife up and drag it parallel to the first cut. Still no pain. Month number eleven and month number twelve. These are the months I have left to be with Punch. When I show him the wounds he'll believe that I can do anything for him. Maybe he'll do something for me.

I stand and watch the blood run down my leg till Bill comes in and starts licking at my shin. He gets blood on his whiskers. I'm making a mess on the floor. I take handfuls of paper towels and swipe at Bill's snout. He takes off. My leg is starting to throb. I press the towels on my thigh and wipe up the floor with the other hand. The blood keeps coming and I get another handful of towels. I'm wishing Punch would get home, but I know he won't. I don't know what made me do this.

I sit and put my foot up on the chair. I press hard with the towels without letting up for a long time. Finally the stream of blood slows. I go to the bathroom cabinet to get some gauze to wrap it up. When I pull out the gauze roll, I see my box of tampons behind it. Seems like it's been more than a month since I've used any. Birth control isn't normally a thought because Punch rarely comes inside of me. I don't feel any different from usual – it's Punch's fault I got the heaves. My tits sure haven't swelled. I get that old scared feeling I recognize from high school, what if? – then I think. It doesn't matter if I am pregnant. I'll be dead before it's even noticeable – the big fringe benefit of the whole plan. Just one more line on my autopsy that nobody will read. It's so simple when there aren't any options.

My leg's throbbing and I'm glad for the pain. I deserve it. I need to test myself, to be tough. I lie down on the couch and try to get Bill to curl next to me, but he won't.

I wake up to the phone ringing, dim light in the room.

It's Isis. "Tell me where you live. I'm coming over there," she says.

"Why? Aren't you working?"

"I need to talk to you. I'd like to come over there."

I look around me, then at the gauze on my leg. It's soaked through with blood. I wonder if she's psychic. All of a sudden I realize just what I've done. It scares me.

"Everything's a mess," I tell her. "Can't we talk on the phone?"

"I'd rather come there."

I give her directions and hang up. I don't know whether to put on my jeans or start scrambling to clean up. I figure the tight jeans might rub open the cuts anyway. I rewrap my leg tightly. I have one dress that's just long enough to cover.

I take glasses to the sink and throw some clothes in the laundry basket. The phone rings. Isis is already at the gate. I buzz her in and step onto the porch to direct her. I make sure not to lift my arms too high and raise the dress above the gauze bandage.

She kisses me on the forehead and sighs.

I lead her inside. "I don't have any tea. Diet Coke? Orange juice? Rum?" I say.

She motions me next to her on the couch. I sit and she takes my hand. "Punch came to the shop looking for you. He was drunk, almost unable to walk. He thought you were upstairs in my bed. He didn't believe me that you weren't." She looks at me like she's trying to make it sink in. "He said it didn't matter. He wanted to watch us – "

"Shit. I'm sorry. I never told him anything. I swear – "

"It doesn't matter. I came here because I want you to get your things and come home with me. I know all about the robbery. I read the story in the paper. As soon as I saw Punch again I put the whole thing together – another of his insane ideas."

I shake my head. "I know it's crazy. But I can't leave Punch. I told you all about that."

"Juliette, you can't stay with him. It's too dangerous. You can't run around town pointing guns and committing robberies. If you don't care about yourself, what about other people?"

"The chefs are happy making us food. They're getting good publicity."

"Juliette, you're young. You don't want to do this. None of it. If Punch has ruined his life that's his problem. Putting yourself in the same position doesn't help him. He's already had twice the life you have anyway. It's not fair of him to ask you to die."

"He never asked me. It's my choice. I told you I can't live without Punch."

She sighs. I see tears in her eyes. "Is there anything else I can say or do to convince you?"

"No. I'm sorry."

She stands up. "At least, visit me once in a while. Just for a cup of tea. I won't push you. You need somebody to talk to."

She puts her hand on my temple and smooths the side of my hair back.

I put my arm around her shoulder, rest my head. "I appreciate you trying to help me. But I can't leave Punch."

She drops her head and takes her hand down. She moves me away. "What's that?"

I look where her finger is pointing at the bandage. Blood has seeped through. "A cut. It's okay."

"What did he do to you?"

"Nothing. I swear. He hasn't been here all day."

I turn to walk away but she grabs my hand and stops me. She squats down, unwraps the gauze. "These cuts are deep." Her voice sounds angry, almost hysterical. She looks around the room. "He used a knife, didn't he? Juliette? What's the matter with you? Do you really want to live with someone who slices you up with a knife?"

"No. I don't. I don't ever. That's the whole point, Isis. I did it myself."

Her shoulders twitch and goosebumps rise up on her white forearms. She stares at me. No doubt she has a good understanding now.

"Let me take you to the hospital. You need stitches."

"I don't need stitches. Scars don't matter."

"Great Goddess on earth, what can I do?" She wipes her eyes. "I'm not giving up on you," she says.

"You should."

She tilts my chin up. "Do you want a spell to relieve your pain?"

I shake my head. "I did it. I deserve it."

She stares at me. "I'm not giving up."

I watch her svelte shape as she strides down the path, loose silk pants billowing. It's almost like she's wading through a cloud. I wonder how strong her magic really is.

18

◆◆◆◆◆◆◆◆◆◆◆◆◆◆◆◆

That night I eat cold cereal and watch one cooking show after another with my leg up. I'm looking at the chefs today, more than the food, the kind faces, sweat on the upper lips, sensitive fingers julienning a carrot, stuffing a salmon, nudging a pink tenderloin into place in the pan. I'd like to be there, in a restaurant kitchen, maybe as an assistant watching and learning. It might be interesting. I rewrap my leg and drag myself to bed.

In the morning Punch isn't beside me. I feel queasy. I get up slowly and hold my breath as I walk into the living room. He's there flat out on the couch. His color looks normal. I feel his cheek. He's asleep.

I walk into the kitchen and sit, groggy and without energy. I feel alone, even with Punch right in the living room. I peek under the loose gauze on my thigh. There's some dried blood on the outside. The cuts are crusted over but still juicy. It aches so I walk carefully and make a piece of toast. I start the coffee pot and sit down to wait for it. I hear Punch go into the bathroom. He comes out with his glasses on. As usual, I'm not wearing anything, and I see his eyes go right to the bandage. It's still clean.

"Hey, sweetheart," I say. I stand on my toes and fling my arms around his neck, push my cheek against his.

He doesn't peel me off, so I know we're okay. I step down and hug him hard around the chest.

"Sit," he says. His eyes go to my leg and he jolts. He shakes his head, trying to get a grip. "I didn't do that. Couldn't have – did I?

"No." I don't know what to say. I can't make sense of it today. "I – I cut myself."

He lets out a groan. "Christ Jesus! Let me see that."

I take my time unwrapping it. I hold out my arms, but he doesn't step close for me to hold on. "I'm scared. You don't think I love you. You don't trust me anymore. I had to do something. I love you so much I want to die – but you don't believe me."

He's watching me, unblinking, his eyes with a hard shine.

"I was trying to get your attention – I had too much rum. But it's okay – I'm okay. I know it was stupid."

He covers his face with his hands. He's crying and he doesn't want me to see. Finally he throws his hands away. His face is red and wet. He grabs me by the shoulders and pulls me up against him, bends and scoops me up and buries his face in my neck.

"I just want to be with you," I tell him. I'm sobbing. "I'll do whatever you want. You're right – I have to remember how to be wild. Just don't leave me by myself."

"God. Fucking life! Juliette, I don't want you mutilating yourself for me. Promise me . . . Christ." He takes my hand to his mouth and kisses it hard, and holds it with his eyes closed like he's praying.

"I have to take better care of you." He picks me up under the thighs, takes me to bed and lays me down carefully. He takes my arms one by one and looks them over like they're the most beautiful, delicate things he's ever seen. He holds my hands to his chest then folds my arms across my stomach, pulls up the sheet. He scoots down next to me carefully and puts his hand on my cheek.

We rest like that for a while. I'm sweating under the sheet, but I don't want to move, ever. I close my eyes and fill with love. Punch whispers, "I never wanted to hurt you. I love you to death, babycakes." He softly turns my face toward him. "Promise me you'll never hurt yourself again."

I nod.

"Suffering isn't in our plan, sweetheart. Understand?"

"Yeah. I know."

"We're going to beat the system – all the fun, excitement, and none of the pain. No more pain. Okay?"

"Okay. I don't want to suffer," I say. "I just want you." The desire is so true, and strong, and impossible, it hurts as I say it, grinding like broken glass in my stomach.

He wants a doctor to look at me, so we put on our clothes and go to the hospital. "See, we need the car," he says.

I get twelve stitches in each cut and a tetanus shot. The doctor asks how it happened. I say it was an accident, on two sharp pieces of metal sticking out on the car. I know he doesn't believe me.

When we get home Punch says I should lie down again for a while. I'm not tired, so I ask him to talk to me. I might as well get something out of my stupid cuts. He makes a drink and sits down next to me.

"Did I ever tell you about the fox?"

"Nope."

"This is just a memory – a weird one – from when I traveled around Europe."

"I wish I'd have been with you."

"Me too, babycakes."

"I would have loved all the different foods and riding the train from country to country."

"I did a lot of that. Drank some good beer in Germany and wine in France. Enjoyed myself all around."

"Where was the fox?"

"The fox was in Greece – Athens, at the Sunday market. A friend and I – "

"A woman?"

"Yes."

"Pretty."

"I guess. I met her along the way. She played the flute. We were having lunch and drinking big bottles of Amstel – "

"What'd you eat?"

"I don't know. Octopus probably, some taramasalata, tzatziki, dolmades. You get the same stuff everywhere."

"Mmm. I'd like to go to Greece."

"It's beautiful. You should."

"I'm going wherever you go, Punch."

He shakes his head. He kisses me.

"Go on," I tell him.

He grunts. "We were at an outside table near the street. This old, beat-up, camouflaged Gremlin pulls up. No doors on it. Two guys get out. Could've been terrorists from the looks of them, but one goes inside the taberna and the other one parks himself on the hood of the Gremlin. He has a small, live red fox on his lap."

"Geez. I never knew a fox would let you hold him."

"Neither did I. Not only did it sit pretty, the guy went to kissing it on the ears and the head, and it held perfectly still. Gradually this lunatic worked his way around and kissed and caressed the fox's wispy little fucking snout. There were a bunch of international tourists there and Greeks, so nobody knew if anybody could speak their language. We all just looked at each other and shrugged and laughed sort of half-assed – "

"Didn't anybody try to stop him?"

"No. It was too fucking weird to figure. Then it got better –

or worse, depending how you think about it. He started licking and sucking the fox's paws, one then the other – had his lips all the way up to the first joint. Then he managed to get about half a dozen tongue kisses in the fox's mouth – before his friend came back with a carry-out."

"Fuck. I think I'd have been running over there, telling that guy to knock it the fuck off."

"You speak Greek?"

"No. I would've done something."

Punch rolls his head on the pillow. "Not a good idea. Anyway, why? It wasn't anybody else's business. Maybe it was love."

"Sure. I bet the baby fox didn't like it."

"Who knows? You would have shrugged it off the way the rest of us did. It was a unified international gesture."

"You know what, Punch? In all your stories you end up shrugging."

Punch laughs. "You're right. That's how I feel about the world – most of the time. It's better than anger, isn't it?"

"Yeah. Why do you get so angry now?"

He gives me a look and I wish I would've kept my fucking mouth shut, but he's not drunk yet, so he drops it.

He picks up his empty glass. "I'm going to do some writing. If you're not up for the dash and dine tonight, I'll handle it."

His going alone panics me. "Hey, I'm not gonna use a couple scratches for an excuse."

He tells me I better take a nap so I'll be able to keep up with him. He tucks me in with the sheet even though it's hot.

"Can I be your baby fox?" I ask him.

"You're my beautiful baby fox."

He gets up and I close my eyes.

Later when I wake up, there's a vase with three red roses on the nightstand. On my stomach is a small box of pastel candy hearts with printed love words.

I go to Punch at the computer and give him a big hug that

almost knocks him off his chair. I smell the heavy scent of rum,
but he stops working and kisses me back. "You're so sweet," I
tell him.

"I'm a son-of-a-bitch. It's all from the Seven-Eleven."

"The roses are beautiful – anyway it's the thought."

He takes me onto his lap. "Someday you'll figure out how
much I love you. Even though I'm a prick."

That night we do the Rooftop Cafe. The chefs recognize us
and laugh. Punch barely aims the gun, just swings it around a
little. I'm getting relaxed. We come out with a shrimp and crab
cake, goat cheese salad, goldust grouper, and lobster medallions.

It's the same routine at La Te Da's a couple nights later. I
order baby greens salad with walnuts and Stilton cheese, black
olive soup, and curried shrimp. The chef insists we take a piece
of his chocolate decadence. It's made without flour – the richest
chocolate I've ever tasted. It even stays pretty in the box on the
ride home. I'm starting to think I could live this way. It doesn't
seem real.

Each day Punch reads the front-page piece about us out loud.
In the La Te Da article they call us "Burrito Bandidos."

" 'Burrito Bandidos?' " I fake insult and laugh. "I wouldn't
bother with a burrito."

" 'Grouper Bandidos' doesn't get it."

There's a continuation of the article on page six. The Chef
from Square One is quoted as saying he's sure he'll be next.

Each time Monty has gotten us information on the layout.
He's either worked at these places or has friends that he visits.
He thinks we're a hoot. Punch's Spanish is getting better and I
throw in a word or two. I go by in the afternoon and check the
menus outside so I have my choices all ready. I choose for Punch
too because he's not particular and always shares.

I tell Punch we could fake having a gun by now – with our
reputation as folk heroes and the chefs loving it. But he says no.
You never know when somebody might want to share in the

fame. Except for pointing the gun, it doesn't feel like a bad thing we're doing anymore. We're almost obligated to cover all the fancy places, so nobody feels left out.

There's no effort to catch us. They must be giving us plenty of time before they call in their reports.

There's an article on Bagatelle the next day that says we got enough food for a party. We get a big kick out of that since we haven't even been there. It's a big old house and no way to handle it. So many gourmet restaurants, so little time. I'm thinking when we're finished, I could send the *Key West Citizen* my list of best heisted carry-outs. But sometimes my selection doesn't hold-up well in transit. It wouldn't be fair. Punch says if he knew more about food he would write a regular column.

One of my first choices of where to go was the Pier House. Finally Punch gets the details from Monty.

"It's a little tricky," he says, "located in the hotel complex, but Monty and I figured out how to do it."

I'm all excited about seeing the Pier House kitchen, since the place has been around so long. I'm into this restaurant stuff, all the sweating and wild food-flipping. I like to check out the equipment, set-up, and techniques. I have a whole imaginary kitchen plan – how I would arrange things if I was going to open a place. I even have a menu with appetizers, soups, desserts. Punch helped me do it on the computer. It's a mixture of cuisines, lots of seafood and spicy dishes, recipes I've figured out from watching and tasting and some real ones from the Food Channel. I would be the chef and Punch could be the bartender, when he felt like it.

"I'd put tables outdoors, so pets could come," I tell Punch, "clear glass tops so you can keep an eye on their fuzzy butts, and they can look up."

Punch chuckles. "That would be pretty cruel making them watch you eat, don't you think?"

"No, I'd have special pet-plates that come free with every dinner."

"I suppose Bill would be the maître d'."

I laugh. "You got it."

I tell him "Juliette's Key West Conch-Coctions" would be the name. He says it's too long to fit on a sign, too hard to say. But hell. It's all talk. I'm no gourmet chef. I just fantasize. I haven't even cooked since Pop died, except breakfast once in a while. Playing around with ideas gives me something to do in the afternoons. We only have six weeks left and sometimes I don't feel like thinking about it. I keep hoping one of my ideas will make Punch want to live long enough to try it out.

I put on my jeans for the ride to the Pier House. I'm sick of the whole costume, but it's our trademark. My jeans are getting tight with all the rich food, so I leave the top button open. The T-shirt covers it. Punch says I'm looking great with a little meat on me, but that I could still use more. He means tits.

We lock the bikes on the side street by the fence. Monty has told us about the delivery entrance closest to the kitchen. We put on our stuff and go inside the maze, taking the turns like he said. We wander down the jungly path past the pool and a cage of cockatiels. There's a bar and then the deck with outside tables. We can see the glassed-in restaurant, but Punch can't decide which doors go to the kitchen.

"We can't linger," he says, "or we'll draw attention."

Finally he chooses a door and we step into a short hall. Punch holds up the gun and we round the corner, Beretta first, into what should be the kitchen – it's not.

It's the main dining room, all elegant with coral tablecloths, aqua tapestry chairs, orchids, candles, and napkins folded like rabbits. It's about a third full of people, mostly older. A woman looks at us and screams. Punch freezes, then walks forward slowly. I tug on his shirt for him to stop, but he doesn't act like he feels it. I follow him, not knowing what else to do. He stops

at the first table, an old couple in fancy dinner clothes, still on
their salads. Punch seems to be in a trance.

The man pulls out his wallet and slaps it on the table. "Here,
here. This is all I have on me." He looks at his wife, "Honey,
give him yours. Hurry up."

She makes grumbling noises and fishes in her bag until she
comes up with a gold wallet that she puts next to his.

I'm still pulling on Punch's guayabera, but I know it's no use.
We're doing a real robbery this time. By choice or accident, I'm
not sure.

Punch picks up the wallets and puts them in his pockets one
at a time, fumbling with each. He's moving slow. I'm really
nervous. I want to get out of there. He shuffles toward the next
table, and I get an idea. I figure we can do this once and then
we'll be finished. We'll have cash, so we can throw out our
costumes and stay a legend in restaurant history.

"Esto es un robo!" I yell. I haven't seen *Butch Cassidy and
the Sundance Kid* twenty times for nothing. "Contra la pared!
Las manos arriba!"

Nobody budges. I wonder if they're going to ignore me. I
know some of them speak Spanish. Maybe my pronunciation is
that bad. Punch looks at me.

Somebody yells, "Against the wall!" A stampede starts. They
scramble toward the far corner, waiters and all, knocking over
some chairs and wine glasses. A guy with a tray comes through
double doors on the right and lets out a little high-pitched shriek.
Punch motions him over and he sets the tray down and goes.

I don't know whether I'm playing Butch or Sundance, but
I'm into it. I whisper to Punch to keep everybody covered while
I go for the wallets. I stand way back behind them so one at a
time they have to stretch to reach me. I work my way from one
side of the line to the other. The people hand over watches and
jewelry too, but I shake my head no. I don't want their things. I
take the money out of the wallets and hand them back. I stuff

the bills all around my waist inside my open jeans. Nobody seems much worse than annoyed. They almost seem sorry for me – I shrug that feeling off. These people are carrying a lot of money, so I guess there's plenty where that came from.

I walk back to Punch. I can tell from his face he's proud of me and surprised. I feel good how I handled myself. I'll have to tell Punch I was inspired by art.

We back on out and I yell, "Hasta luego, bon appétit!" Nobody moves. We turn the corner and run, rip off the clothes behind the fence. I want to leave them, make this the grand finale, but Punch stuffs it all into the bag and we run and get the bikes. I hear a siren a couple blocks away and I know the police are after us this time. We're out of there and racing through alleys before they get close.

When we get home I strip and throw the money down on the bed. Punch goes into the kitchen for a drink and he comes back with one for me too. He looks down at the heap and smiles.

"How'd you like my Español?" I tell him it's from the movie. "I'm life imitating art, just like Key Largo."

"Life imitating art imitating life," he says. "Butch Cassidy and his gang were real people – so were Bonnie and Clyde. Yeah – the book is art imitating life, imitating art imitating life. Like a picture of somebody holding a mirror reflecting mirror images, ad infinitum. We're creating something beyond a simple, single reality."

"Cool. You always manage to top me, don't you, Punch?"

"That's what I'm good for."

Those words are from Butch and Sundance, and I wonder if he knows it.

He holds his drink out for a toast. "To the ultimate couple in crime," he says. We clink glasses. "To art." We clink again.

"To our retirement," I add. I sip my drink.

He clinks on that but doesn't say anything. I can tell by his face he doesn't have the same feelings as I do. There's a knot, like a fist, tightening in my stomach. I take another sip of my drink and set it down. I'm remembering Etta now – Sundance's girlfriend – she wouldn't stay to watch them die. She knew the odds.

19

◆◆◆◆◆◆◆◆◆◆◆◆◆◆◆◆◆

The next day we're covered in both *The Citizen* and *The Miami Herald*. They've got some details wrong as usual, like saying we took expensive jewelry. But there's one real clue – witnesses report that I'm not Hispanic. They could tell by my pronunciation. I'm surprised we got by with it this long.

At least there's a funny article by a gourmet critic in the food section of *The Citizen*. He writes that the food and excitement made a great night out and everybody got their meals complimentary. Some customers saved money since they'd planned to use credit cards and barely handed over enough cash for a tip.

I get a call from Isis. She's read the paper. She's worried and says her offer is still open for me to stay there. She says she got involved in some trouble as a young girl in Massachusetts and understands.

I say, "Thanks. I'd like to, but I can't."

"You're too smart to waste your life," she tells me.

I know she's wrong, but I promise her I'll be careful.

In the afternoon I'm riding my bike to the liquor store for Punch when I pass the cop again – Woodly. He looks at me and waves. I hold my dress down so it doesn't show my cut thigh.

He's smiling and I know he likes me, but it gives me the creeps, like an odd coincidence. I wonder if he's watching me. Maybe evidence is stacking up.

Later I tell Punch and he says we'll cool it for a while. We've counted up over five thousand dollars, plenty to eat on and do whatever we want. Punch skims two thousand off the top to repair the Triton, and over the next week we take rides to Marathon and Islamorada, and spend a few hours at Bahia Honda beach. Punch only has a couple chapters left on the book and then he'll let me start reading it. He says we're taking life one day at a time. I call it a countdown.

By now I know I'm pregnant because my bellybutton has popped out. I don't have much of a gut yet. Punch mentioned I'm starting to mature and round out finally, but he must know the truth. He's a little softer with me in some ways – or maybe it's just because we're so near the end. But my condition doesn't make any difference if we keep to the plan, so neither one of us says anything. Only thing is, I cut down my alcohol, just in case. I don't know what I'd do with a kid, but I can't think of the scrawny dude inside me getting hungover.

I've been to see Isis, just as a friend, and to visit Moon-cat. Everything's cool. Isis doesn't have a clue about my condition since I wear the loose sundresses anyway. She doesn't bring up anything I've done, just gives me a sorrowful look now and then.

After lunch on October 1st, Punch pulls me down onto the couch and tells me it's time to do another job. "Not for the money," he says. "We need to go out with a bang. If we up the pace we can be on CNN by the end of the month. With all the advance publicity, somebody's bound to publish the book. We can leave all the money for charity."

"What if we get caught? Go to jail? We won't be able to get the book published."

"I have it all set up." He stops. "You know I'm not going to prison."

"Neither am I," I shout. My throat tightens. I know how serious he is. I catch hold of myself. "But it's dangerous," I say. "Somebody innocent is going to get hurt. We don't need to take any more risks."

"Everything carries risk, babycakes. Every time you drive a car you risk killing somebody – and maybe you're only going to the movies. How necessary is that?"

I know we're near his point of "interesting," and there's not enough time to spend it arguing. I need to think. I wipe my eyes. "I guess we're doing the Robin Hood thing now, huh?"

Punch kisses my forehead. "Exactly. Think of it that way. As Helen Keller once said, 'Life is either a daring adventure – or nothing.'"

I smile and take his hand and press my cheek into it. "Isn't there something we can do that hasn't already been in a book or a movie?"

"Afraid not, m' dear. Too many people in the world, too many movies, too many books . . . There's a guy who got published after he committed suicide. He won a Pulitzer – so even that's been done."

He takes my face in both his hands and kisses my mouth. "Let's ride a wild horse into the sun."

"The Trojan horse?"

He smiles – I know you're yanking my chain. "Triton. I was quoting the last line of a poem."

"I figured. You're in that kind of mood."

He shows me a list of several places to hit in the next two weeks, including some where we've already done the kitchen. "They're all expensive enough, so we'll only be taking from the rich," he says. "We don't have much time. We can start with every other night. If we get enough coverage early on, we'll cut down."

"The tourists aren't going to like us like the chefs do."

"That's why we have to move fast, make our hits before the

word gets around and the clientele drops off or stops bringing cash. We might have to do a couple places on up the Keys in between."

20

◆◆◆◆◆◆◆◆◆◆◆◆◆◆◆◆◆

The next job is the Casa Marina. Punch says it's a great location, isolated and easy to get out of. We wear our costumes to build on our reputations. Punch says we should still use a little Spanish, just for charm. I don't know about this CNN idea. Seems to me like Punch should be working on writing, but he says the robberies work for both reputation and inspiration. I'm starting to wonder if our being arrested wouldn't be the best thing. If only we could be in a cell together, I'd go for it.

We ride the bicycles because Casa Marina is so close to home. We're keeping a low profile with the Triton when possible. When we open the door to the inside of Casa Marina, I jerk. I wonder how we're going to handle this room full of people and three entrances. Punch must not have gotten all the information this time. I look at him to object but he nods to me to slip on my mask. He slides his on and puts his hand on my hip. I feel the cold steel of the Beretta.

"Take this gun. Cover the door."

"What?"

"I have my own." He points to a huge shining gun in his waist band.

I recognize it. It's the Colt .45 from Uncle Sam's. "Punch!"

"Do it," he says. He steps inside.

I'm standing in the open door. I go rigid.

A blonde waitress walks by and Punch grabs her arm. He pulls the Colt up and shows it close to her head. She gasps. "Do your job," he says to me.

"I can't," I tell him. My voice is shaking. I remember something he's told me, a deep emotional memory. I'm desperate. "Think of your grandfather. He wouldn't do this."

Punch gives me a strange look. Threatening. People scream.

I want to turn and leave, but I can't. It's too late. I get that out-of-body feeling like I'm in a movie. It's a scene I've watched so often. It's not real. I turn and cover the door.

"Everybody, into the back. Put your hands up and walk fast or she gets it!"

In less than a minute, he gets them faced to the wall. I wonder who's going to collect the money, since I'm guarding the door behind him, but he yells instructions and everybody starts dropping wallets and purses on the floor. "You – " he points to a young woman in an off the shoulder black dress, "Take out all the money and bring it to me."

"Yes, sir. You're the bandidos, right?"

He nods.

She looks a little scared, but works fast and almost cheerfully.

I look back at my door just in time. A woman and a man step inside. I point the Beretta. I know the safety's on anyway. "Back against the wall," I yell.

Punch angles toward them, so they can see exactly what's going on, and they both let out a noise and hurry to the back.

I take a breath and keep my eyes glued to the door. In a couple minutes the young woman brings the money up to Punch in a large bag she emptied out.

"Very resourceful," Punch says.

I think I see her wink. I can believe it. Even with the mask on, the beautiful smooth skin of his jaw and neck are enough to do it.

I stow the money in our pack and Punch backs up toward the door still holding the blonde, just like in the movies. I don't like the picture. The Beretta looks like a toy, but the Colt is mean. It's bad luck. We've gotten away with so much because people like us. We're amusing. I know the Colt is going to change all that.

He gives the blonde a shove and she stumbles forward as he slams the door. We run down the hall and outside, passing the woman at the desk.

We hear sirens in the distance, but the restaurant's so close to home, we cut through the alleys and they don't have a chance at us. All the same, this is serious trouble.

When we get inside, I go to the refrigerator and search through the carry-outs for a pasta dish. I'm starving from all the stress. Punch mixes himself a big strong drink. I know he's ready for several. I follow him into the living room with my carton and sit down on the arm of his chair next to him. I need to explain my feelings before it's too late. He drinks down most of the glass while I'm talking.

"A gun is a gun," he says. "The law is the same, regardless of the size."

"But the Colt's nasty."

"We need to heighten the tension," he says. "We're nearly finished. That's what I'm doing in the book."

"I don't like scaring people to death."

He kisses me on the forehead. "We'll be as nice as we can be. I only have to hold the gun on one person."

"What if you have to shoot that one person?"

"I wouldn't do it. I promise." He squeezes me against his chest and I slide down into his lap. I feel the gun still at his waist just like in the movies. It makes me shiver, even in his arms. "You can't leave me now," he says.

When he gets to that, I give up. I hear the tinge of rum hitting home already. There's nowhere to go and no way I can stop this.

He finishes his drink and gets up. "I'm sorry," he says. "I'm not my grandfather. I gave up on that a long time ago."

He goes into the kitchen and I go out on the porch and light up a joint.

In a few days we do Cafe des Artistes. It has a good set-up and we manage easy. I move delicately through the elegant furnishings and take very little money. People smile at me and the waiter hands me a carry-out of shrimp with mustard sauce. They're special – divers get them from 800 feet down. I'm starting to feel better again. We're so well-liked, I'm thinking maybe even the looks of the Colt can be ignored. Punch sends compliments to the chefs in the kitchen – saying the food looks so good he wishes he had time to eat.

We get lots of news coverage, " 'Burrito Bandidos' Strike Again" kind of stuff. Somebody got a picture, but only our costumes are recognizable.

The next day the police report that they're ready to start random stake-outs. I tell Punch it's time for a rest. We should enjoy some dining as normal customers. But he insists we need a few more jobs. We can spread northward to throw them off.

He's on the couch and I climb onto his lap and lean against his smooth chest. I've got a new idea. I tell him it's time to give back some money if we're really doing the Robin Hood thing. We have a backpack of money stowed under Albin's house with about six thousand dollars in it and another four in the closet. It's a waste. I'm thinking we'll either be dead or – in my fantasy – the book will be bringing in lots of dough. "I don't feel right spending stolen money," I tell Punch. "Besides, we can put some niceness back into our reputation if we let people know."

"Name it," Punch says.

"We can leave the money at Albin's and pass out the hundred-dollar bills from the closet. That's my idea for tonight."

"We can't hand them out in person."

"Course not. We'll leave notes."

He kisses me on the forehead. "Sure, babycakes," he says. "I don't know why I didn't think of that."

I spend the next hour writing out greetings on sticky notes to put on the bills. "Yours for an evening out." "Enjoy!" "Have a nice day!" "Spoil yourself." I don't know if people will really report the money – maybe they'd have to give it back. But the reputation isn't really important. It just feels like a nice thing to do.

We wait until early evening and take a leisurely walk to Bahama Village. It's a little rickety compared to the commercial quaintness on Duval Street, but I like the small white and pastel painted wood houses and quiet sidewalks. It feels like a real tropical island.

Blue Heaven is down the way, and we haven't eaten there for a long time since we got to be so fancy. It's one of my favorite places, so we stop there for dinner before we start our money run. We sit at a table under the trees and listen to a poet reading into a microphone. Punch is drinking beer, I'm enjoying the food, and the chickens are running around in the grass under the tables as usual, but I feel a sick, sad feeling take hold. I can't stay happy for long anymore. I feel like I'm wasting time whatever I'm doing. I finish most of my grilled fish and rice, but skip dessert. It's dark.

"Let's go deliver the money," I tell Punch.

I have twenty-three hundred dollars in my purse and Punch keeps a look out while I sneak up to each house of my choice and put a hundred with its sticky note in the mailbox or under the edge of the doormat. Punch stays in shadows on the street. I feel like it's Halloween when Pop would take me door to door. For three years he dressed me like an angel. I remember that and now I don't like it. He stuffed me into that costume after it was way too small.

I pick houses with flowers, cats, toys, or tricycles outside and ones with cute curtains. I'm afraid to try the homes with dogs. I try to get a feel for which places would have nice people that need a surprise.

At a wood-frame house on the corner there's a little girl, maybe four or five, sitting on the porch step by herself. She's delicate and pretty, and in the porchlight her skin has the deep caramel glow like Punch's. I can't help thinking – wondering about the color of the tiny body inside me. She's singing to herself and twisting a braid. She's freshly dressed in red-checked shorts with a white top and red plastic sandals and I wonder if she's waiting for someone to pick her up. I know I shouldn't go over there.

Punch sees me hesitating and motions me away.

I pretend I don't see him. I have five or six hundreds left and I dash up the walk and put them in her hand. She looks at me with big clear eyes and curls her plump fingers around the money. A sticky note falls off. I'm standing there in clear view and I don't know what she'll do, or who might show up any second. I want to give her a hug, but I don't dare. I dart back to find Punch. He's already moved around the corner.

I take his hand and pull him into a run down the street. We run four blocks. I'm out of breath but full of energy. I grab Punch around the neck and hang onto him, kissing his face and head. I nearly drag him down with my weight because he's not expecting it.

"That was great," I say. "You're such a sweetheart to let me have all the fun."

He smiles and hugs me back. "I wish we could do this always, babycakes," he says. "If only this were the real world."

"I don't see why not," I say. "When the book gets published

we'll be able to do whatever we want. We can give away a little money whenever we feel like it."

Punch smiles and looks into my eyes. He turns my chin up and kisses me. "You're so beautiful and innocent," he says. He takes my hand and starts walking. I know he isn't giving a single thought to what I said.

21

◆◆◆◆◆◆◆◆◆◆◆◆◆◆◆◆

The next night we ride north on the Triton to Islamorada to hit the Green Turtle. We park the bike in the bushes a little down the road. As soon as we open the inside door of the restaurant I feel bad. It's a dark dining room, kind of old-style with a wood bar, glasses and bottles glowing behind it, a nice atmosphere. The customers are mostly regular tourists, not the fancy crowd we've been heisting in Key West. They look scared and I feel like a criminal. I wish I was having a bowl of the turtle soup instead. It smells delicious, a rich, sweet, biting aroma. I don't even get a taste. Punch seems to have forgotten all about the food part of these gigs. I only take a twenty off of each person, enough to make it a hold-up. I'm thinking this is getting too easy, and our luck is bound to change.

We move fast back to the bike and onto the highway toward Snapper's. Punch says the last thing anybody would think is that we'd go straight to another restaurant. We park down the road and walk around back to the bar. Snapper's is another friendly looking crowd. I don't like robbing people in shorts. They probably work hard and saved their money all year for this vacation. I whisper to Punch, "Can we just eat? I'm starving."

He gives me his sharpest look and pulls out the Colt to point
it at the barmaid. He pulls her out to the side. A young waiter
down the bar starts crying.

"What's your name?" Punch asks the barmaid.

"Mary. Who are you?"

"Tell him you're all right," Punch says. He nods toward the
waiter.

"I'm fine, Ricky," she says. "Just be quiet and we can get this
over with."

Punch points to the drinks on Ricky's tray. "Have a slug of
something," he says. "I'm not hurting her. See, I'm very nice." He
glances at me to make sure I see.

Ricky takes a gulp of beer and quiets down. We get everybody
behind the bar and I go down the line, wondering when Punch
is going to catch on to my sneaky ways. I'm robbing and unrob-
bing the folks, trying to get the large bills back into their wallets.
It takes longer than usual.

"Hey, Burrito Bandidos, hurry up! Our filet's getting cold,"
some guy yells. When I get to him, he opens out his wallet and
shows six dollars and credit cards. He laughs like he's pulled a
big one over on me.

"Keep it," I say. "This is all for charity. You seem like a
charity case."

When I'm finished collecting, I stop at a table with a fresh
basket of gator bites. I'm nearly fainting from hunger. I dip a bite
in sauce and pop it in my mouth.

"Uno más," I yell to Punch. I eat another one then toss a
plate of half-eaten shrimp to the fish hanging out under the dock.
The water churns up in the feeding frenzy.

Punch shakes his head and I know his eyes are rolling behind
his mask, him thinking how cocky I'm getting. Really I'm almost
numb about the idea of getting caught. I'm so sick of this.

He grabs a fifth of rum on our way out and we run behind
the trees on the side road to hop on the Triton and race off.

We're finally heading back when we hear sirens getting close. We turn onto the old highway into a dark spot and they go by. Punch takes out the bottle of rum and sips on it. We happen to be right next to Old Tavernier, one of the best restaurants I remember from when we first stopped on our way to Key West.

"Let's forget the costumes and go eat. I'm dying for a good relaxing meal," I say. "By the time we get home nobody will be serving."

"I remember this place," he says. "It's too good to miss. We owe them some publicity."

"I just wanna eat."

"You can get a carry-out."

"For Christ's sake!" I say, but I'm so wrung out I can barely speak. I just follow him.

We have to go up outside stairs to the second floor so it's a bad set-up. We make our entrance. Punch pulls out the gun, grabs his hostage, and starts a sweep to the rear. A waitress has just put down a tray in front of me. I walk back and get a couple carry-out containers by the register.

I dump a garlic-crusted lobster tail and a blackened tuna steak into the boxes and put the little rolls dripping with garlic and oil on top. I set the stuff carefully on top of the money already in my backpack.

Punch is standing there with the Colt out, but the noise level is loud. Two people have knocked each other down and others are joining in yelling.

Punch looks at me. "Shit, we need to get some respect here."

Before I can say anything, he shoots a lamp out in the corner. The glass splatters on the wall. I jump and grab his side. A woman close on our left starts screaming. It's piercing, louder than the gun. She doesn't stop.

Punch points the gun at her. The hostage ducks away. I'm scared. The woman screams louder and I think it might be driving him insane. It seems so easy to pull that trigger.

"Punch," I say. I take his shoulder and step in front of him. Our eyes meet in the slits of the masks. The woman stops screaming. "Okay," he says. He pushes me aside and points into the crowd that's still lined up in the back. "Get the money."

"No. Let's get out of here," I tell him. "There's no room left for more money."

He looks and sees the carry-outs filling up the knapsack. He shakes his head. "Get a bag."

"Punch, we have to go. Somebody could call the cops from outside and we'd be stuck up here."

He stands there rooted. I grab his arm and pull backwards toward the door. "Come on."

Finally he moves with me. We fly outside and down the stairs. I can hear the hubbub start behind us.

We roar out of the parking lot and head south. I feel a rush from having made it out of such a tight spot.

We fly back doing seventy, yipping like cowboys over the bridges, pretending to whip our horses, feeling the wind. I nibble part of the lobster tail, shielding myself from the wind behind Punch's back. By the time we get to the cottage, I'm beat. I'm not even hungry for the rolls.

"I hope that's the end of it," I tell him. "We've done enough. We're taking too many chances."

"I wasn't going to shoot that woman," he says.

"I know," I say. But I don't know for sure. "We have plenty of money."

"We'll take a break," Punch says. "Just one more big hit – the night before Fantasy Fest."

22

◆◆◆◆◆◆◆◆◆◆◆◆◆◆◆◆

I wake up with a terrible feeling the next morning. I think it's from a dream, but I can't remember anything. I look beside me and Punch is still asleep. Then I know what it is – in exactly one week we'll be dead. We haven't talked about the particulars lately. I know Punch has enough sleeping pills for both of us. I see the bottles every time I open the bathroom cabinet. I picture us painted black with glow-in-the-dark bones, the two of us heaped together on the float, people laughing and pointing.

I wonder if Punch needs to take more of the pills so they work on us at the same time. I don't want to go first. I don't want to go last either. I'm afraid it's impossible we'll be able to die exactly together. One of us will have to hold a dead body.

I don't think of gourmet food in my stomach anymore. All I can do is hope that Punch finishes the book and changes his mind at the last minute. I won't live without him, but death is too real now to joke about. We'll have to drink plenty. I'll need to be as drunk as Punch. At least there'll be no pain – for us or the critter inside me.

I roll over and put my arms around Punch. His skin is soft, smooth and warm. I don't want to think of anything else.

I move down and put my mouth around his cock. It's a rubbery button in my mouth. I suck at it, pull it with my lips, roll it with my tongue. He's not moving, trying to make me think he's asleep, so he can let me work on him a long time without seeming selfish. But his cock is growing and his hips have tensed up. They're not dead weight, not yet.

He's gotten big and he can't pretend anymore. He touches my head with his fingers and smooths my hair back. I'm up on his mouth instantly. I stare at his face, the lines and crinkles on his cheekbones, his dark eyelashes. I feel his tongue and the thick slippery insides of his lips. My arms are tight around his ribs. I crush myself into his body. I want him so bad, not the sexual parts, all of him.

He puts his arms hard around me and I can feel he's desperate too. It's past sex. The feeling grips the insides of my stomach and makes my chest fill with a hot ache. We hold each other, our ribs and hips sealed together, sweat pouring and making our arms slip into place, like folded wings on each other's backs. We're like two insects in one cocoon.

We hold on as long as we can. I'm being crushed. I don't care. I want it. I'd rather be smothered into Punch and die now, never let go. I hang on as long as I can. My body takes over and I loosen up and throw my head back for air. Punch follows, slinks down. We fall deeper into the bed like we've been tight on the surface. I can feel the love packing my chest. The muscles in my back twitch.

Now looking over at him, I see what Punch looks like, clearer than ever before, even though I have every crease and blemish memorized. I have the supernatural feeling he tells me about. I don't want us to die. I let myself imagine for a few seconds that we could live and have the baby.

Punch gets up for his insulin and gives himself a shot while I watch. When he's finished he sits back on the bed and counts out six more needles and swabs and throws the rest away into the red plastic disposal box. "Doc told me I would never be able to stop using this gear." He laughs. It's a hollow scary sound.

Bill comes in and hops on the bed. I take him against my chest and rub his bony head. "Do you have any more stories, Punch? I don't want to miss any."

"You just want to keep me in bed."

"Why do we need to get up?"

He reaches out and tickles down my thigh and traces around my kneecap. "I was thinking about what you said. How my stories always end in shrugs. It made me think of the first time I came to Key West – before I met you."

I pull him down on the pillow next to me and roll on my side against his chest with my arm across his stomach. He puts his hands behind his head and looks up at the ceiling. For a second I feel like we'll be doing this over and over for years. Then I sink back into the truth. "Talk to me, Punch," I say.

"It's no story, just a short incident. I had my car and was driving down Duval – around the south end."

"Did you have somebody with you?"

"Nope – that'll be clear in a minute." He looks at me and rolls his head. "You never change, do you?"

"Not some things. Want me to?"

"No, m' dear. Anyway, I was stopped at a traffic light and a beautiful woman waved to me and stepped off the curb."

"You were probably staring."

"No, I just looked. She was obviously a hooker – all made up, bleached hair, short short vinyl skirt, great legs. I had the windows rolled down and she came around to my side. Before she got close, I could see stubble on her chin and upper lip."

"Italian?" I ask. I laugh.

He reaches down and smacks my cheek. "No, smart ass, transvestite."

"I know. I'm teasing."

"She – he – sticks his head in the car and says, 'How 'bout a little blow?' "

"Blow job?"

"I would assume so – unless he was selling coke. I didn't ask him to clarify."

"What'd you do?"

"Just told him I'd take a rain check."

I giggle. "Typical." I kiss him in the armpit and rub my nose into the hair until he howls and squirms and pushes my head away. I laugh. "And you shrugged."

He shrugs. "I don't know. I had that shrugging feeling. I think that's the night I decided I could fit in down here if I ever got the chance – at least for a short time. Whatever blows your skirt up, you know?"

"Sure."

He grabs my butt cheeks. "Anyway, there's more – speaking of Italians – my Italian grandfather had a saying. When he'd see a really obese, unattractive woman walking down the street – "

"With a mustache?"

"Get off it." He smacks my ass again. "He'd say, 'Attsa somebody's queen, Punchinello. Attsa somebody's queen.' " Punch chuckles. "I'm sure he never knew the full meaning of that statement in Key West. He died when I was in my twenties, but I always remember that. His whole attitude – you don't come across it too often."

"I bet that's why he let your mother marry your father – you know, in Tennessee, in those days – "

"He had a basic respect for all human beings. I admire that – that's something I admire about you."

"Me? You never told me that."

"Lots of things I never told you."

"Like what?"

"Things that can't be told."

"Tell me. Please. I don't want to be scared of what they might be."

"Scared? How can you be scared, Jul? You only have a fucking week till you kill yourself."

He's trying to put me off the idea, by coming out with it so strong. "Oh, Punch. Fuck," I say. "That's why you should tell me."

"Just good things, m' dear. Trust me." He strokes back my hair and traces down my eyebrows to my cheeks, to my chin. "I don't have the words to tell you. Good things. Trust me."

I see that glaze come over his eyes and I know he wants me. I move over him. "I don't wanna think anymore, do you?"

"Uh uh."

Bill jumps off the bed and I get my legs on both sides of Punch and lower my face slowly, staring him in the eyes. I suck his lips one by one and pin his arms where he has them behind his head. I nip his chin. I pull my head up. "If you don't have the words, then you're gonna have to show me," I tell him.

He lifts his wrists off the pillow like I'm not even holding them and pushes me back. He climbs over me and I see he's getting hard already, without even touching. He kisses my neck and moves down my chest and then moves back up again to my mouth. I'm craving to be filled up and then I feel it. I feel him sliding into the wet heat inside me. He's so hard and big, I don't remember it ever like this. It's a solid burning that moves up my body till I feel the sweet pain in my chest and arms, and my head is tingling. Then the tingles cluster behind my eyes and turn to tears. I cry. I cry because it feels so good. I cry louder and harder because there won't be much more.

I feel tears dropping on my chin from Punch above me. I look up. His face is twisted in a look I've never seen before. He's, like, not there – he's elevated – yet he's there, in pain. I know this because I feel it myself, the blend of heaven and hell, and they're both the same, the best, worst feeling I guess I'll ever have.

Punch starts sobbing along with me. I grab his hips and dig my fingers into him and he pounds against me harder and harder. I feel explosions inside, clouds in my head, flames around me. Our crying turns into shrieks and his face is a blurred shadow above me. The room glows red. Then it's over.

I feel a flow inside, like the tide going out, taking all my energy. I never want to move again.

Punch rolls off me. He leaves his hand on my stomach. "We can never do that again," he says.

I look at him. "Why not?"

"It's not possible. Something like that can't happen once, much less twice."

"Huh?"

"Besides – it'd kill us."

I know he's making a joke, but I don't laugh. I let myself drift off, wondering if we could go out of the world locked together in deadly ecstasy.

When I wake up, Punch is watching me with his head propped on one elbow. "Guess it's time to rise and shine," he says.

"I can't think of anything else I want to do, besides lie here with you," I say.

"In a week that's all you'll be doing – somewhere."

I know he's trying to impress that, working on changing my mind.

"Get up. Eat. Drink. Take a few thousand bucks and go buy some crazy knick-knacks – I have to keep writing. It's the one important thing. You know that."

"I know. All I want to do is help you. I don't want to shop."

"There's nothing you can do here. I'm stuck and I need to work my way out of it. Think of something you like. Make yourself do it." He puts his shorts on and stands ready to step out the door into the living room. "Do it for me."

"Everything I do is for you."

"Just think, you're free to do anything – totally free."

"I don't feel free."

"Did you ever hear of Diogenes?"

"No."

"He was called 'the dog' – a philosopher in ancient Greece. He lived like a dog out of doors, owned nothing, needed nothing but the crusts tossed to him, answered to no one."

Bill comes back into the room. Punch bends and scratches him behind the ears. "We're free, just like that, but better. Our time is short, but we have everything – temporarily. Now go enjoy it."

I know "go" is the important word here, but it's not easy. I grab his leg. "Punch, we never figured out what to do with Bill. We can't leave him here to starve."

"That's true. Now you have a job. I'm going in to write and you figure out what to do with Bill."

He bends and kisses my forehead and I let him go.

I fix us some eggs and toast and then take my shower. Punch is working the whole time. His fingers barely stop.

I put Bill on his leash. I stop on my way out the door. "I'm going to find him a home. I want to make sure he gets settled."

"Uh huh."

I bring Bill over. "Say goodbye to Bill."

Punch looks up at me, then down at Bill. "You're taking him already?"

His eyes start to fill up and he looks back at the computer. He knows I want him to stop me.

"I'm going to try Isis, but I don't know. She has the cats."

He reaches down and pets Bill on the rump. "It's been real, buddy," he says. He puts his fingers back on the keys and turns away.

I kiss him on the side of the neck and turn. I look back.

He shrugs.

I follow Bill out the door.

23

◆◆◆◆◆◆◆◆◆◆◆◆◆◆◆◆◆

I walk Bill a little ways down the street to sniff and piss and then bring him back. It's too far for his little legs to Isis' place, so I put him in my bike basket. He settles down like he's been trained to ride. I wipe tears out of my eyes. I'm still thinking there's a chance to change Punch's mind and I can always get Bill back from Isis.

I see her through the window as I carry Bill up the steps. She's beautiful in a flowing white dress and dangling silver earrings. I tie Bill to a porch chair and go inside.

Isis looks up surprised. She smiles and puts down the wands she's arranging.

"Hi," I say. I walk up close to her so she can kiss me on the forehead. I hug her back. "I'm sorry. I have another favor to ask."

"You never ask much, Juliette."

"Can you take Bill? He needs a good home."

She puts her hand across her eyes and shakes her head. "How about you? You need a good home."

I drop my head. "I just need to find a home for Bill. Will you take him? I know I can find a nice tourist at the sunset, but I would like you to have him, if it's possible."

"You know I'll take him. I just want you to tell me why you're giving him up."

"You know."

"I want to hear it. I want you to hear yourself."

"You believe we're all masters of our fate, don't you?" I ask her. I remember seeing that on one of the books she sells. I point toward the bookcase.

"Yes. That's why you need to think for yourself."

"I've thought. You want me to say it? I'm going to kill myself on Fantasy Fest night and I don't want my dog to be locked up in a cage or put to sleep."

"Juliette, you can't do this. I won't let you."

"You told me you don't interfere with fate."

"It's not fate." She stiffens and puts her head back. Her arms go out straight, her fingers clench.

It scares me, like she's being crucified on an invisible cross. I don't know what powers she's calling up. Tears flow down her thin cheeks. "Don't do this, Juliette. I know what you're feeling. My lover, my soulmate – she was depressed. I couldn't help her. Before I realized she needed a doctor, she overdosed. I wanted to die too after that."

"I'm sorry."

She shakes her head. "No. Be happy for me. I didn't die. Things change. Now I thank all supernatural powers that I didn't do it. I've found many good things since then. One of them is you – as a friend always."

I'm trembling. I know what it was like for her. It all becomes real to me, how I would feel without Punch. I start backing away. "I'm not as strong as you. I can't live if Punch dies."

She sighs and hangs her head. "I should tell the police that you're the ones robbing the restaurants. I should have done it already. You'd have a hard time killing yourself in jail."

"I don't want to go to prison."

"I'm really only thinking of you."

"Then don't tell. It's almost over."

"I know. That's the problem." She comes closer and hugs me hard. I can feel the pulse in her neck against mine and her breath catches like she's sobbing inside. I feel myself gripping back. She holds me until we both settle down.

"Let me do one more spell on you," she says.

I nod. I don't even ask what kind.

She brings Bill in and I give him a bowl of water. We go upstairs and I throw off my dress. I need all the magic I can get.

Her eyes open wide when she sees my slight roundness and popped-out navel. "Oh, Great Goddess," she whispers. "Why didn't you tell me?"

"I figured it was another thing to upset you."

"I don't know what to say. I can't believe you're still following that nightmare plan. Everything's changed."

"Nothing's changed. You really think that I could be any kind of a mother? Support myself and a baby? It's nuts." I blink back tears. "I don't want a kid growing up like me."

"There are many options." She stops and looks me square in the face, presses her hand on my hard stomach. Her eyes get hopeful. "I would help you. I could even take the baby."

I see how serious she is and it makes me feel terrible. "I would give you the baby right now, if I could."

"You can live to give birth. You can do whatever you want. It's all in your power."

She goes to the circle and begins lighting candles. I watch her knowing I'm not worth the trouble. I'm not the good person she thinks I am.

She brings me into the circle and kneels in front of me. I feel a tingle and smell her scent. She focuses on my stomach. There's a tiny movement inside. I don't know if it's real or imagined. I wonder if the little guy can sense something through my body.

I feel my warmth for Isis growing with her words and touch.

I've found a trust I've never had with anybody. I know she's thinking of the good for all.

When it's over, I slip on my dress. Isis puts out the candles and comes to stand beside me. She takes a deep breath and I know she wants to say something, but she doesn't. She seems ready to cry.

I put my arm around her bare shoulders and press my cheek against hers. "After Punch, you'll always be the most important person in my life. I love you, Isis."

I leave there feeling desperate. I could almost go home and close myself in the bathroom to swallow the fucking pills so I don't have to think about it anymore.

When I get to the cottage, Punch is still pecking away. He looks at me and his eyes are bleary. From booze probably, not overwork. I wonder if the words he's typing make any sense or if it's something like – all work and no play make Punch a dull boy.

I go into the bathroom and just for the heck of it, check the medicine cabinet. The brown prescription bottles are still waiting there, for us permanent sleepers, no more worries, no more memories. I sit down on the toilet and listen to Punch out there typing. The plastic clicking noises are getting to me. He's working on the book and I'm just waiting.

I decide to do one more skin-show on Catherine. What the hell? I'll watch my ass. I bet no pregnant woman has ever paraded herself on Catherine Street before, not in a book, not in a movie. It will be all mine, one last fling of my own, the showing of the biggest tits I've ever had. I'll do a survey. This time I have a plan.

I go into the kitchen and eat some fairly recent risotto. There's still a big collection of leftovers in the freezer, mostly Punch's. I open a beer and take a few swigs and put the can back in the refrigerator. I don't take the Beretta, too risky now.

I walk by Punch and out the door. He doesn't say a thing. His fingers never stop. I don't look at the screen. I'm realizing that the whole flashing routine is pretty tame, since I've become a bandido by night, but it's my own crazy thing. I'm only wearing a thin sundress. I feel myself juicing up. The pregnant female flasher on Catherine Street – if it doesn't work for the book, maybe Jimmy Buffet will write a song.

I find my spot on Catherine and sit down on the wall, light up a joint. I decide to keep my dress on until the last second, in case of a Woodly encounter. I'm keeping an eye out for his bright blond hair.

I see my first participant, a young dark-haired guy. He looks familiar, probably a waiter. He's walking fast so I jump out in front of him and lift my dress up to my neck. It's white and I figure it looks like angel wings in back.

"Dear, dear," he says.

I can tell instantly that he's not the type I'm looking for. I give it a try anyway. "I'm doing a survey – what do you think of these tits?"

He puts his hand to his cheek. "Honey, I have a guy friend with bigger titties than yours." He points down to my pussy. "He doesn't have one of those, however. But who would want one?" He laughs and walks around me. "I'm late for work," he says. "Have a good day."

I don't say a thing. It was bound to happen. I let the dress fall and sit down. I need to pick more carefully.

Next come two guys together talking and gesturing. Not worth a try. I suck on my joint. They don't even glance at me when they pass.

I wait ten minutes and nobody comes by. Finally I see a few people walking from the direction of Duval. There's a woman and behind her a couple. The woman is ahead some distance.

I wait until she passes and step out to get a good view of the couple. Seems like an interesting twist. They're definitely tourists, both in Margaritaville T-shirts, carrying bags.

I get behind a bush. They're talking and laughing. I jump out and flip the dress.

"Jesus," the woman yells.

"This is my costume for Fantasy Fest," I tell them. "How do you like it?"

They both stare.

"I'm taking a survey – what do you think of the tits?" I pinch a nipple.

The woman rolls her eyes. "Let's go," she says.

I look at the guy. His eyes are roving up and down. She takes his hand and hurries him off.

After that, I flash two separate guys. The first one just laughs and keeps on walking. The second one giggles and pulls down his pants to moon me. It'll do.

There are long waits in between and I start to get bored with the whole thing. Just like Pop used to tell me – I'm boring. That and I'm going to end up like my mother. The bastard – saying those things was mean and threatening. Why didn't I ever tell him that? He drove Mom away – to her death – and substituted me. That's how it was. I know it. It's always been clear, if I'd have taken the time to think. Pop and his fucking little doll. I always felt sorry for him that he was stuck taking care of me. I guess that's what he wanted me to feel, so he could treat me however he wanted – put his fingers wherever he wanted.

I feel a wave of heat and anger, but it passes fast and I'm relieved. He's gone. I can do what I want – for a couple more days. Fuck. I take a last hit of the joint, burn my fingers, and drop it. Everything's meaningless unless I can convince Punch to give us some time.

Shit. I need something so quirky to happen that Punch will want to rethink our whole plan. I wipe sweat off my forehead. It's tough to be unusual in Key West.

I'm ready to wander on home when I see somebody coming my way. He's big like Punch and dark-haired, in a muscle shirt and jeans, watching the ground almost angrily as he walks. I decide to make his day. I step behind a bush so I can jump out and startle him.

I listen as his footsteps on the blacktop get closer. I push the dress up and over my shoulders so it looks like a white neck scarf. I step out.

I halt. I'm two feet in front of him. I smile. "Ooh," he says. He takes my wrist, looks down my body. "What's this?"

"I'm doing a survey," I say. I twist my arm to get loose, but his fingers clamp like steel. "Let go," I say. I feel a flutter in my stomach.

"Not yet," he says. "Ask your questions, little girl."

The tone of his voice sends sparks of fear through my brain. I look over his shoulder to see if anybody's coming, but the street's empty. "Let me go. I was just flashing you."

"Flashing me?" He laughs low in his throat. "I like that. Interesting girl."

I'm in a hot panic, but I notice the word interesting. Nobody ever called me that. I look into his eyes to see how he means it. They're solid green ice, locked to my nipples. I take a breath. "I thought you were my boyfriend. He's meeting me here."

"Oh?"

I wait for him to look around to check my bluff, but his eyes move from my tits to my crotch. His fingers stay tight on my wrist.

"Oh?" he says again. "He must not be fucking you right if you have to stand around naked on street corners." With his free hand he trails a finger down my jaw to my collar bone. "You're lucky you found me."

I feel my eyes opening wider, but I don't want to scream and give him a reason to shut me up. I jerk my head to the side, look over his right shoulder. "Punch, I'm over here!"

The guy glances sideways and I wrench my wrist free and dart left. My dress falls into place and I run past the bush. I'm expecting a hand to grab my hair any second, but nothing happens. I pick up speed. I can only hear my own crunch on gravel and a rushing sound like the ocean in my ears. I take a turn between the next two houses to get out of sight as quick as I can.

I hop over a low rock wall, scattering lizards like crazy. I dash between some Australian pines through a cluttered side yard and behind a house. I'm breathing hard. My chest is tight. I slow down. Cats are all over the ground, under bushes and in soft spots of grass. There's a high wood fence across the back and dividing fences a couple houses down in both directions. I can't get through to the next street so I'll have to cut back out to Catherine one way or the other.

I catch my breath and walk back along the side of the house and peek around to the front. I can't see him. He probably went on his way, but I don't feel safe walking out to the street yet. I head back to the cats to wait a while.

I turn the corner and smack straight into solid flesh. He crushes my head to his chest and a rough hand slips over my mouth. His weight buckles my legs and he rolls me backward onto the ground. His hand presses hard on my teeth forcing the back of my head into the rocky sand. One arm is mashed behind me, my other hand crushed by his knee, my thighs held by his other leg. I twist and wrench, but he's too heavy. I can't get my body out from under him.

With one move he unbuttons his jeans and slips the zipper. His big cock spikes out. I feel the air so I know my dress is caught up above my hips giving him a clear target. I see movement out of the corner of my eye – but it's only cats moving up closer, watching.

He pins my arm with his hand and moves his leg to center himself. "Nice cunt," he says. "If I had more time I'd eat you. I'd eat your ass too, huh?"

I look into his icy green eyes. My mind is numb to him.

"I bet you like to be fucked in the ass."

I squint and gather all the coldness I have to stare back. I twist my shoulders and wrench my hips an inch or two off the ground.

"That's pretty." He licks the corners of his mouth. "Relax," he says. "You're about to get the fuck of your life." He lowers himself and slips into me on the first try.

I feel him hard and tight. I know I'm wet even though I hate him being inside me. I feel every stroke, but it's not pleasure. I'd like to break off his prick and shove it up his ass.

I want to say hurry up, get it over with, ass-hole, but his hand stays hard on my mouth. I wait while he pumps, thinking how I brought this on myself, how stupid I was to think I could control any situation.

The bastard on top of me is grunting and sweating. A trickle runs down his jaw. I can't tell Punch anything. He'd say I was stupid. He'd never forgive me. It makes killing myself sound easy. I can't keep a secret like this between us.

He lets out a deep groan and lowers his hips on me. His hand relaxes on my mouth, but I don't feel like moving. I think about the baby under him and the nasty come inside me, the baby's tiny pink toes wiggling in it.

He takes a few breaths and smiles. "No reason for you to tell anybody about this. I didn't hurt you, and I don't go around grabbing chicks on streetcorners." He blows at a leaf on my nipple. He takes his hand off my mouth and brushes the leaf away. "You wanted me. That's why you lured me back here. You needed a good fucking." He puts a hand on my jaw and holds my head to look me in the face. "Yeah. Did you good. If you make up some lie, you're not gonna fool anybody, not even yourself."

I nod. Even if I wanted to tell Punch and report a rape there's Woodly and all the other people who've seen me. Any of them could be witnesses on his side. I took my chances for trouble and found it.

"You give me a few minutes before you come out to the street."

"Okay."

He lets go of me and gets to his knees. I straighten my dress and sit up. I watch while he zips and buttons, stands and brushes off his knees.

"Haven't had enough?" He laughs and takes my hand and pulls me up next to him. My legs are so shaky he catches me under the arms and lowers me back to the ground.

"You sit right here and play with these nice pussies for a while and you'll be fine. When I'm gone all you'll have is romantic memories."

I sit there numb until he's out of sight. I drag myself up and walk. When I get home, Punch is sitting on the couch with a rum and coke waiting for me. He pats the cushion next to him for me to sit down.

"One second," I tell him. I run into the bathroom to pee and rinse myself off. I look in the mirror and notice that my bottom lip is a little swelled. It's cut on the inside from a tooth. I'm pale and sick-looking. I check my elbows for dirt and pull my dress around looking for grass stains. There aren't any noticeable.

"Your friend was here," Punch calls. He sounds part tanked. "I think he was hoping for another shot of your furry little bush, but he missed out."

I step out of the bathroom but I'm shaking, so I walk past him into the kitchen and call back, "Who?"

"The cop. Two people reported you."

I gulp down a glass of water. I wish Woodly had found me – maybe if I'd screamed. "It must have been a tourist couple. I should've known." I walk back into the living room and stand there. I'm feeling limp.

"That was a crazy thing to do."

"Isn't that the whole idea, to do crazy things? I wanted to do something original – for the book."

"You could get hurt. I mean it. Look – I can't just put in some weird incident anyway. I'm tying it up. You let me figure out what has to happen."

I sit down next to him. There's a cloud of rum fumes between us, so it's likely he won't notice I'm still shaking. "I don't care if I get hurt. Why should I? It doesn't matter anymore. Soon we'll be dead. Nothing to worry about."

"I'm not going to discuss it. You just stick with me. I don't want you thrown in jail."

"I'm going wherever you go."

I look at his soft smooth face. He shakes his head and drops it sideways onto my shoulder. I can't ever tell him what happened. I'm lucky he's too drunk to notice that I'm talking through a tight throat and my lip is puffed.

"I won't do it anymore. I'll never step out the door without you again."

"Good girl."

He takes my face in his hands and nibbles my mouth. He holds me like I'm used to, like I want forever and I'm thinking right now might be my whole forever.

"Suck on my nipples. Please. I need to feel loved."

He looks up startled, like he's just realized something.

"Please. Be my baby."

He pauses then lifts my dress and puts his lips on my nipples and closes his eyes to suckle. I take his head in my fingers and stroke his thick hair back to hold his ears. There's no milk, but I feel a warmth that's different from other times. I feel safe.

He moves from the right nipple to the left and I crush his face against my pounding heart. His hot tears squeeze out on my skin.

The next morning we're drinking our coffee and Punch finds a tiny headline on a back page of the *Miami Herald*. "Female

Flasher in Key West," he reads. "A young woman, described as a blonde in her late teens, wearing a white dress around her neck and nothing else, was reported on Catherine Street near Duval yesterday. Police were called to the scene, but the woman was not found."

"I had on flip-flops," I said. "They never get it right."

"They noticed you were a blonde." He reaches down and tugs my bush. "Hmm. Little girl flasher – also a famous Burrito Bandido. Great publicity if they put it all together. Maybe I could work in a scene somewhere."

I get up for the scissors, to add this to all the clippings that we're saving to put with the book for when we're gone.

"When can I read the novel?"

"Soon. You'll read it. Don't rush me."

I want to say that I won't be around, but I don't want to get anything started. I stand up and grab his head and nuzzle my face in his hair. He opens his mouth and kisses the skin on my belly. I'm wondering if the little creature inside knows it's being kissed and if Punch is thinking that too. I wipe my eyes. My stomach growls.

Punch lifts his face. He's staring into space. "Fuck. I don't even have a reversal."

"What?"

"Just thinking out loud – about the book, babycakes. Where I'm at right now. Whew. I know what I have to do." He puts his hand on my stomach. "Let's see if they have the eggs Benedict florentine at Camille's today," he says.

"Sounds good," I say. I'm thinking I can count on one hand how many breakfasts I've got left.

24

◆◆◆◆◆◆◆◆◆◆◆◆◆◆◆◆◆◆

We decide on Louie's again for our last hit. Punch says it'll make a good finale to end where we started. The Triton is ready to go. This time we'll eat first then change our clothes and come back for the money. I tell Punch it's going to be hard to enjoy the food when the tension is on, but I'm willing to give it a shot.

"I'm sure you'll manage to choke down a soup, an appetizer, and an entree," he says.

"Maybe a dessert too," I tell him. "I hope they don't think we dislike the food when we pull out the gun and all."

I slip on a sundress and put the other stuff into the backpack. Somewhere else it might look funny, Punch with a backpack, in a fancy restaurant, but not in Key West. We have a reservation for eight, when they're sure to have a crowd.

We walk in like regular customers. I take my time and look around. There's a reception area with little trees in pots and a window seat, wood floors and wicker furniture with purple velvet cushions. It looks cozy, like somebody's expensive home. We're led up the few stairs to our table and I run my fingers over the tropical tapestry on my comfortable chair. Candles in black metal holders glow on white tablecloths and make the glasses sparkle.

Our table is by the glass walls overlooking the balcony and three decks of dining areas. I can see the waves rolling in under the last one, the backyard Louie's is named for, a perfect setting for a romantic evening, not a robbery. I can see the dog beach to the right and there's one unescorted dog digging a huge hole.

Punch points to the tables outside under the trees. "We'll move all the bar patrons and these people in here. We can lock the entrance and keep the back covered. Nobody out front will be able to see what's going on. By the time they figure it out, we'll be gone."

"Should've brought a sign saying 'Private Party,' " I tell him.

He shrugs. "We can handle it. We're good."

The waitress hands me the menu and introduces herself as Kim. We order our drinks.

I look at the fancy food descriptions. "I can't decide on my appetizer – whether I want the Norwegian smoked salmon and golden potato terrine with Maytag blue cheese, roasted peppers, basil-infused olive oil and Osetra caviar or the Maine lobster and brie lasagnetta with toasted hazelnuts, pancetta and spinach."

"For Christ's sake, get them both."

"What's Maytag blue cheese?"

"Beats me. Aged in a washing machine?"

I laugh and grab his knee under the table. I scan the entrees. "Do you think citrus-scented basmati rice tastes like citrus or just smells like it?"

"Fuck if I know. Whatever it is, my palate's not that sensitive. Why don't you order me something?"

That's just what I've been waiting for. The waitress comes back with the drinks. "I hope you can handle this," I say. "It's going to be a big one."

"Have at it," she says.

I pick my two favorites out of each category. I know Punch

will give me the onion-rosemary potato tart that comes with his roast rack of Australian lamb and I can have the horseradish encrusted grouper with pickled tomato-chili butter sauce.

"Let's get an extra entree," I say. "I have to try the spinach and chèvre strudel with the New Zealand venison loin."

"You're crazy," he says.

"You just figured that out?"

The waitress is laughing. I look up at her. "Think we can fit everything on this table?"

"If not, we'll just scoot up another one."

I laugh and she goes off. That's about all it takes for me to get sad as usual, because I'm having such a good time and soon it will be over. Kim will be up against the wall with everybody else.

Punch sees it. He tilts my head up with his fingertip. "You shouldn't get so friendly," he says.

I blink and he picks up his drink and guzzles it.

When the appetizers come, they're art. I work on everything and Punch eats a few bites. He's drinking very fast. He has four rum drinks before the entrees are served. I'm getting nervous. I've had enough before I've eaten a quarter of all the stuff.

"Let's get this over with. It's wonderful, but I'm ready to go."

We ask for the check and to have everything wrapped up.

Kim wants to know if everything was all right.

"Great," I tell her. I don't want her to feel bad. "I'm pregnant and my stomach's weird."

Punch twitches. I know he really couldn't have missed it before. Maybe the sound of the word in public just surprised him. It did me.

Kim brings back the leftovers and they're made into beautiful foil peacocks, a whole flock of them in a plastic bag. "It's art inside art imitating life," I tell Punch.

He smiles a little dopey and I'm wondering if he's ready for the main event.

"We don't have to do this. There's no reason," I say.

"I have no expectations. I have no fears. Therefore, I am free. That's from *Zorba the Greek*."

"I have fears. We've done enough."

He sighs. "I need one more scene. I want to end with Louie's."

"Please just make it up."

He shakes his head. "I need inspiration, baby. Don't let me down."

I frown and reach across the white tablecloth to take his hand.

He kisses my fingers. "That's my babycakes."

We pay the check and leave a huge tip. "Let's make sure Kim keeps her money," I say.

We head out the door and there's nobody around. We turn left onto dog beach and crouch between a bush and the restaurant to put on our disguises.

"Vámonos," Punch says. He tromps up the ramp to the Afterdeck Bar to grab a waitress and herd the diners toward the inside. I take a gulp of air and run back around to watch from the front.

I slip on my mask and step inside. There's a commotion already. The diners are looking outside to the back toward Punch.

"Burrito Bandidos," somebody yells. I feel the thrill run through me, that cheap high like I get when I hear about us on the news.

The front bartender and maître 'd are standing there looking up toward the dining room.

I draw the gun and holler. "Vámonos, amigos!"

This gets their attention.

"Who has the keys?" I yell.

They look at me, but don't move.

"This is loaded," I tell them.

The bartender takes an attitude. He rolls his eyes and reaches under the bar. It scares me for a second, but he holds up the keys. "Lock the door," I tell him.

He follows orders and I motion them up the stairs into the main dining room where Punch has everybody pressed together, hands up on the glass walls to the right.

"Put your hands on your heads and join the crowd," I tell them. I step over broken glass and an overturned table to cover the back entrance.

"Drop your cash," Punch hollers. "Give it up for charity."

I can see as far as the water and nobody's coming that way. I go down the line and collect the wads of bills that are being flung on the floor. Kim is there and throws down a handful of cash from her pocket.

"Not you," I tell her.

She looks at me and I see she recognizes me from earlier, but that doesn't matter now. I retrieve her money and put it in her hand.

"Thanks," she says. "I need rent tomorrow."

I have all the cash in the bag with my birdie-wrapped dinners and I grab a handful of bills and stuff them in her pocket. Her eyes are big. I move back to stand near Punch and the hostage.

"Okay," he says, "Nobody move."

We walk left and I push open the glass door with the wrist of my gun hand. Punch turns to walk through and just then I see a movement to my right. Punch sees it too.

A guy is hunched behind an overturned table. His hand rests on the edge with a nice-sized handgun pointing straight at me. He's frozen like that. It flashes in my head that Pop is going to be right after all. I'll be floating in a ruby-red puddle real soon.

Punch moves his arm to center on the guy's chest. We're only twenty feet apart and I know Punch is loaded in both ways. Their eyes are locked. I picture us dead on the floor. I can't move. Punch knocks me aside and a blast rips my ears. Then another.

I cringe and turn. The Colt blocks out the room with its size. Punch is standing rigid, holding the gun in both hands. I look at the guy. The gun is gone and he's on the floor, his upper body

thrown out from the end of the table. He's clutching a shoulder
of blood. Blood runs through his fingers and down his arms.
There's blood splattered on the white tablecloth and a puddle is
spreading on the polished wood floor. I'm trying to figure out if
he got hit on the side with his heart, but my brain won't work.

"Now we've done it, babycakes," Punch says. He looks like
a zombie.

I see blood oozing down the side of his pantleg. "Jesus!"

Punch follows my eyes. "It's okay. Let's go."

The hostage starts screaming, and Punch holds her harder
against him. He starts to back through the door. "Come on!
Now!" he yells to me.

I go ahead of them to keep the way clear. I've got the Beretta
out in front of me and I'm feeling numb.

We turn outside and run to the bottom deck. Punch pushes
the hostage into a chair and we take a right down the ramp
onto the dog beach. The Triton is where we put it. I ball up our
masks and shirts and stuff them in the plastic bag.

The noise is loud as Punch accelerates and we tear off, right
turn on Waddell and a tight left on William. We're zooming for
fucking hell, if there is one. I'm holding on for dear life – scared
to death I'll die today, even though I've vowed to kill myself
tomorrow.

Punch is zigzagging – right on South, left on Grinnell, right
on United. I hear sirens toward Duval. It's the ending of Bonnie
and Clyde and Butch and Sundance all together. I realize
Pauline and Papa are long gone. I feel the wind and smell clean
salt air, but I know it's over no matter what we do now.

We come to Watson and lean left for home, but Punch straightens the bike out fast. I see the cop car sitting in the lot – they
know who we are. Isis, I'm thinking, trying to save me.

The cops see us and back up. Punch hangs a turn at the next
street and we're out of sight before they reach the corner. The
siren shrieks on. We can out-maneuver them on the small streets,

but I don't know how long before we're trapped. Where can we go in Key West?

We snake through more alleys and side-streets until we're running north, parallel to Duval on Simonton. I hear more sirens from every direction. I look behind and all around, trying to catch a glimpse of which direction they're coming from. Everything's out of control.

We make a left on Angela right before the police station and head toward Duval. The sirens are hurting my ears. We pass the witch shop. I imagine Isis near the window watching us go by in the scream of sirens. I smile in case she can see. I want to let her know I don't hold anything against her.

I expect a cop car at the intersection, bullets splattering our bodies, us wiping out and scraping off all our skin on the pavement. But there's no cop. Just the one a short way behind us on Angela. Punch makes a right on Duval into traffic. I can't figure out where he's headed, not off the island, maybe nowhere. He snakes through cars and onto the sidewalk and the cops are out of sight again.

We go left on Front Street and cut through the parking lot toward Mallory Dock, slowing up into the swarm of tourists gathered for sunset. I don't know if this is Punch's plan or if it's just luck we happened on a crowd to get lost in.

Across the parking lot on the dock the performances are in full swing. The tightrope walker Will is silhouetted against the orange sky under a heavy layer of dark clouds, and to the right, a trained housecat makes his leap through a fiery hoop.

Punch parks the bike. As I hop off I hear the bagpipe music although I can't see the piper in his plaid skirt. It's eery, like funeral music floating from far out at sea. I hustle along beside Punch toward the dock. We're headed between the tightrope walker and the trained housecats, blending into the weird entertainment, like nothing's real or it's déjà vu. Maybe a dream.

We hustle toward the water among the tourists. I'm watching for the cops to come through the crowd any second.

"Now we've got a chase scene – for the film," Punch says.

I realize he's talking about the book – a movie version. We're both in other worlds.

I bump against him and feel the hardness of the Colt he's holding under his shirt and the fantasy is over. We dodge the cookie lady on her bicycle and slither through the crowd behind the performers to the edge, about ten feet above the water. Punch pulls me down beside him to sit on the raised piece of concrete. We hunch there at a dead end, nowhere to go. "Whatever happens, I have to finish the book," he says. "I just need one more day."

I hear how desperate he is, and I try to think what we can do, how we can hide, now that the cops know who we are.

I pull his arm across my shoulder and press against him. "Maybe we can go to Isis' place," I say.

He stares at me like I should come up with something real.

I shrug. It's not the don't-give-a-damn shrug, like Punch's. It's my don't-have-a-clue, but I catch a glint in his eye and smile, because I know he thinks I'm imitating him, putting a carefree shrug at the end of our story. He smiles back, and we both start shaking with laughter, because it's such a perfect ending – our whole loser lives in a nutshell, on the concrete edge, with everything closing in, all exactly what we set ourselves up for.

Punch gives me a kiss and I feel his tongue in my mouth. We hug and hold each other and start to laugh out loud, through the tears. I see people staring but I don't care. I feel drugged. My head is light. My face is streaming with tears and snot.

The sun goes behind a cloud, cooling the glare, and I look up. I glimpse Woodly to the left, getting close. He's ducking down, working his way through the crowd. Besides all the usual commotion, people are scattering. He's holding his gun.

I wipe my face on Punch's shoulder. I look to the right and there's another cop, moving in from farther off. I scan the crowd and I can see the uniforms of others, bright white shirts, six or more, some with the little hardhats they wear when they ride bicycles.

Woodly brings the gun up. He's either aiming or clearing a path. I stiffen and Punch turns.

"Drop your gun!" Woodly hollers. "Give yourself up!"

A man stumbles and blocks Woodly. I feel Punch going for the Colt. He pulls it up. He's shaking. I know he's going to shoot out of fear.

I have to take action against him. I step in front of the Colt, facing Punch, staring into his eyes. He grips my shoulder like he's going to fling me out of the way, but I feel a rush of power flow from my guts, a tingling that strengthens and hardens in my arms and legs. I hold my ground and jam my hand against the evil hole in the muzzle of the Colt. The metal shines in the setting sun. I push as hard as I can, feel it slide, put my whole body into it. It clicks.

Punch looks at me in shock. I put my hand down. I turn to look behind me. People are scrambling and dropping on the ground and Woodly is holding his gun on us. I look back and see Punch fidgeting to take the safety off. He steps away from me. He's holding the gun down low. I don't know what he's doing.

"Drop your weapon," Woodly yells.

Punch hesitates.

I have to finish it. No choice or Punch will be shot. I make a rush into his side with all my weight and knock him off balance toward the water. He reaches for my dress to hold on, but the thin fabric slips through his fingers. I can barely hold myself back. He catches my eye as he goes over. He splashes down. I feel his hurt in the most surprised and saddest look I've ever seen. A few drops of water fly up and hit my legs. The Beretta drops from my waistband onto the concrete. I've betrayed him, and it was the right thing to do.

The sun peeks from under the cloud, an orange yolk just

ready to disappear. The dazzle spreads across the water. I can't see Punch. Woodly steps up holding his gun on me and takes my arms behind my back. I look back over the side. Punch is swimming to the fenced-off cruise ship dock about twenty feet out. He grabs the bottom rung of a steel ladder. The Colt is gone from his hand. He doesn't try to climb up. I wonder if he lost his contacts when he hit the water.

Woodly puts heavy metal handcuffs on my wrists while another cop picks up the Beretta. He makes a call on the walkie talkie and others keep the crowd back.

Woodly takes my shoulder and moves me away from the edge. He looks disgusted and sad. I walk past the knapsack on the ground where Punch dropped it. Money and foil peacocks are spilled on the concrete. A cop hunches next to the pile, getting ready to gather the evidence. He picks up one foil bird. I blink. Its head and tail are squished down and it looks just like a dove with folded wings. I think of Isis and a tingle runs through me.

The breeze picks up and I smell the garlicky sauce and remember Punch's tears on my neck, and our last laugh. I wonder if I'll ever see Punch again.

25

◆◆◆◆◆◆◆◆◆◆◆◆◆◆◆◆

In minutes the police boat roars up to get Punch. Woodly walks me through a path in the crowd. I stumble along. My legs are weak. When we get into the parking lot a camera zooms at my face from the side. As wiped as I am, I smile to beat the world. Woodly guides me towards a car.

We get to the station and I'm taken upstairs to an office. Punch isn't anywhere around.

A detective comes in and tells me I have the right to a lawyer, but I say I'll answer their questions. Nothing to lose – as planned. There are plenty of witnesses anyway. I'm thinking maybe I can get some sympathy for Punch.

I tell them the whole story of how we started so innocently, just being an amusement around town, and never planned on any shooting. The other guy drew his gun first. I tell them where the money is in our closet and under Albin's house, and that we weren't going to spend any more of it ourselves, just give it to the needy. I can't stop myself. I let out everything about the Hemingway House gig.

The cops put me in a car and drive me to Stock Island to the Monroe County Jail. They won't tell me anything about Punch.

I'm numb as they lead me in and almost too tired to stand. After more paperwork I'm given a jumpsuit to wear in exchange for my costume and led down a yellow hall that reminds me of my old high school. The guard puts me in the first cell and I don't see anybody else. The place is hollow. It's a tiny concrete room with a small bunk and a grungy sink and toilet, just like in the movies. The grey walls are scratched with names, I-love-you's, and mostly fuck-you's. The guard clanks the door shut and leaves me.

I lay down and close my eyes so I don't have to see anything. The air conditioning is cold and the mattress is hard, cracking plastic. I huddle into it and cover my face, but I don't cry. I feel like a rock, unable to move. I keep picturing Punch, what he might be doing. He'd probably be needing a drink bad by now. I picture his cold eyes. He's thinking about me and how I got him caught by the cops.

I start to sob because I know he'll never understand my going against him. I mash my face into the mattress so nobody can hear. I cry until there's no water left in me. I fall asleep. I dream we're still on the run, zooming across bridges. Zooming. Zooming. I wake up hot and crazy in the head. I fall back to sleep and dream the same thing over and over.

The next morning I keep my eyes closed until the guard comes to get me. He puts me in front of a TV and I talk to a judge on a special two-way system. He sets bond, so all I need is money to go home. I don't know if Punch will be allowed bail. They won't tell me.

I call Isis. My bond is $100,000 dollars, and I need 10 percent for the bondsman. I'm thinking if she can get me out, I have enough money left in my account for Punch and then I can give her the car and bike to repay her for helping me.

She doesn't sound surprised that I'm in jail.

"I don't have the money for both of us right now," I tell her. "But I can pay you back."

"Don't worry. I have the money," she says. "I know you won't run off."

"What about Punch?"

"I'll ask about him. But – Juliette – I don't think they'll let him out."

"You don't really know anything, do you?"

"No. I just don't want to get your hopes up."

It's two in the afternoon by the time the paperwork is done. Isis leads me to her car.

I wonder if she reported us, but I don't ask. "What about Punch?"

"I tried," she says, "Not a chance with the charges against him."

"You tried hard?" I ask her.

"Yes. I did. I'm sorry. There's no way. His leg wound was slight and that's all taken care of, but it looks to me like Punch will be held until he goes to trial and serves his time."

Tears fill up my eyes. "He won't last that long," I tell her. Reality hits hard when we get into the car. I don't know what I'll do by myself. I'm cold and empty. I wish I was still in jail.

Isis wants to take me to her house, but I say no. I can't keep talking. I want to go home and close my eyes and turn into a rock.

She works on my head all the way back from Stock Island. Tells me she'll help me and I'll be fine with the baby. Tells me everything will be better now that Punch is under control. Nothing I haven't already heard or thought about. But I know it's all impossible.

We get close to the turn off toward the cottage. I can't wait to shut myself inside. "If you won't take me home, let me out here," I tell her.

She turns.

She parks the car and follows me through the gate to the cottage. I open the door to more than the usual mess. Cabinets and drawers are still open from the police search. There's a form on the table that shows they got the money from the closet.

Isis straightens a drawer of paper and computer discs. She gives me a glass of ice water. "Why don't you come visit Bill?" she says.

This makes more tears run, but I shake my head no. I just want to get into bed. I'm still cold from the jail.

"It's my life. I have to live with my choices," I tell her. "Don't worry about me. In a while I'll go down to the parade."

"You're not still planning . . .?"

"No. I won't ride the float without Punch. I just have to watch. He might need details for the book."

Finally she stands to go. I give her a hug and she kisses me. I watch her walk down the path to the gate.

I look around at the empty room. The closet door is open and my dresses are on the floor. The thin straps have slipped off their hangers.

I don't intend to fall asleep, but I wake up at dusk. I get out of bed fast with my mind whirring about Punch and our last night, the plan to get air-brushed and do the grand finale. I pass the mirror and see myself with a round stomach. This is the first day I notice it, like it bulged out in the couple hours I slept. I run my hands across the pouch. It doesn't feel like me.

I try to get through to Punch by phone, but I'm told I can't talk to him. I call the police and ask for Woodly, to see if he knows anything. He's not in.

I can't do much after that, not even eat. I curl up on the couch and stay still enough to feel myself breathing. My stomach has a cold ball of steel in it and my throat aches. The phone rings and rings. I know it's Isis, but I don't want to talk. I already know everything she would say.

About eight I drag myself up and put on the gaudy butterfly disguise. I can hardly walk out of there, but I have to go.

I trudge down Catherine to Duval. It's the same as the first time I walked it, in every way but feelings, all a blur of green leaves and streaks of setting sun on the rough gray road. It's the end of October, the end of everything, and still hot summer.

The parade starts at nine, but the street's already closed to traffic. I pass La Te Da's. The restaurant is decorated with a giant pteranodon and crepe paper from porch to roof. Lots of buildings are in costume like the year before. I get a pang of happy-sad feeling from the first time Punch and I saw all this.

The flow of people is just a trickle on the south end, but I can see the hordes up ahead. I walk alongside giant condoms and a voodoo priest and pass groups of slow-walking matronly men in sequined dresses and spike heels until I get into the thick of the crowd, a curb-to-curb mob of skin, fur, feathers, paint, and papier mâché. Everybody is strutting up and down until the official parade. I grab a coke from a stand and squeeze into a spot on the curb in front of Fast Buck Freddie's Department Store with families of tourists and drunks that already can't stand, the ones of us that aren't in the mood to show off.

I see lots of faces I know from around town. I'm not sure who they are, probably local salespeople and bartenders – maybe restaurant customers and chefs we held up. I recognize Skippy the guitar player wearing a safari hat and gear. I remember the theme for the year is "Call of the Wild." I slip my mask on. The last thing I want to do is talk to him – or anybody. After a while the iguana guy passes by in a Tarzan outfit with his albino snake around his shoulders. I think I recognize Punch's friend Monty next. I can't be sure because he's all air-brushed into a golden lion with a mane and pointy ears and a g-string with a tail. He's walking next to a tiger-striped woman with six tits arranged cat-style and the tiniest g-string holding on her tail. I can tell which set are the real tits because most of the paint is rubbed off one of them.

I'm looking for Isis. Nobody else seems to notice me with all the bizarre outfits, but she'd be on the lookout to make sure I wasn't going to take my last nap.

Wizard goes by without a costume, but he fits in okay with his leather vest and tattoos. It's like my whole life – all the important part – is passing in front of me and I don't exist. Nobody recognizes the short half of the Burrito Banditos. If Punch was with me they'd notice. Then we'd be real interesting, get back on the news.

The parade starts and I slump down with my elbows in my lap, too sober to be interested in the floats of semi-nude people celebrating. I don't remember much detail of last year when I was one of them. I know I was hanging onto Captain Tony's float in my mermaid costume with Punch's arm around my waist, waving wildly, thinking if I fell off it wouldn't hurt – just so I didn't spill my beer. That was a week after I left home, when we were rich and free, and I thought a year with Punch was heaven forever.

Some guys in diapers drive by in a red convertible. One guy on the hood isn't tucked in good. I can see his balls and the tip of his penis all the way from the curb. He doesn't care. He's pouring a beer on the crotch of his diapered friend.

A row of six queens swings by in puffy wigs, sequined leotards, nylons, and spiked heels. One's holding a boom box and they're kicking their legs to the music and holding onto each other in a chorus line, but with the size of their shoulders it's more like a football defense.

I watch their little asses head down the street. When I turn back there comes Isis in full black witch costume riding slowly on her bicycle. Bill is in a basket on back, perched like he's a pro. Isis has striped red and white stockings and black laced boots. I didn't know she had a sense of humor about her profession. I'm thinking Woodly would make a good scarecrow, grab Monty for the lion, and Punch for the tin man, and we'd be on our way to a musical. A tear sneaks out – it's sickening self pity.

Isis passes by without noticing me, so I jump up. I dry my

eyes and run beside her. She stops and puts her feet down and
smiles. A clown walks around us.

I take Bill out of the basket and hold him to me. I
remember I missed the pet parade. Bill would look so cute in a
costume.

Isis puts her hand over my hand on Bill's head. "Honey, I'm
so glad to see you. I couldn't get you on the phone. I almost
called the police, but I felt you were all right . . ."

I know she's relieved. I step back for a unicycle to pass
between us. "They wouldn't let me talk to Punch. I slept the
whole afternoon."

"He's better off in there," she says. "He's protected from
himself."

"Maybe so."

A horn beeps and I look behind me to see the start of a
parade pile-up. The Frank Sinatra impersonator Twig waves and
pulls around us in her taxi. Now we're blocking a float of sweaty
jungle people. A high school band is marching in place behind it.

We move to the curb and let the float pass. The high school
band follows. It's too loud for us to talk. Bill starts wiggling his
whole body. I cuddle him closer and he licks my face.

I stroke his little head until the band passes.

"Want me to drop off Bill after the parade?" Isis asks. "He
misses you."

"No, not yet," I say. I can't think of a reason to give her. I
can't think how my life is going to go on. I try to bury my face
into Bill to stop my tears, but he's not big enough.

Isis grabs my upper arm in her fingers. "Juliette, you're not
still thinking of killing yourself, are you? Are you?"

"I'm not thinking of anything," I say. "I just miss Punch."

"Punch is away from the alcohol. He might find a whole new
perspective."

I lie. "I know. I'm okay. I'll talk to you tomorrow. You need
to get back into the parade before it's too late." I put Bill back

in the basket and he keeps wiggling at me. I smile at Isis and wipe my nose on my wrist. "Better get going before Bill jumps out."

She frowns.

I smile and nod.

She stares at me, then looks behind her and sees a gap where she can get in. She bends sideways and crushes me to her thin body, moves her hand down to hold my stomach. "You're going to be fine," she says. "I'll help you." She lets me go and weaves back into the parade.

"Thanks, Isis," I yell. "Thanks . . ."

She looks back at me and I see gloom on her face. I duck through the row of people at the curb and walk behind them down the store fronts toward Catherine Street. I'm not watching where I'm headed. I almost step on the balls of a human penis. He recognizes me.

"Hey, bandido!" he yells, "Where's your old man?"

I cut left out of the crowd.

"Gotta gourmet salami for you, baby!"

I try to throw back a glare, but I can't find his face in the foreskin. I turn onto Catherine and the anguish of being alone settles down on me.

26

♦♦♦♦♦♦♦♦♦♦♦♦♦♦♦♦♦

I get home at ten-thirty and strip off the ugly costume. I throw it on the bed. I don't know what I'm doing anymore. I'm alone with nothing but a promise to kill myself. Maybe that doesn't count anymore, but if I live, I'll have a baby I can't take care of, and I'll either die of loneliness or go to prison. I think of the ridiculous trouble I've gotten into – the trouble I've caused people – and the rape, the taste of his salty, rough palm in my mouth, a total stranger's smug understanding of my weakness. I picture the cats sitting around to watch. They have better sense than I do. I'm worthless.

Punch's jeans with the hole in the crotch are on the floor in front of me. I bend and pick them up, press my face into the smooth worn cloth. I haven't cleaned up for days. The place looks ransacked. I drop the dirty clothes into the hamper, throw away the empty bottles, and do the dishes. I start to sweat. I don't know why I'm doing anything. I don't know what I'll do when I'm finished.

The phone rings. I figure it's Isis. I let it ring. I'm too down to talk. It stops then starts again. Finally I give up and answer. It's the cops outside wanting to be buzzed in through the gate.

My heartbeat picks up. I think maybe I can find out something about Punch. I run outside and down the walkway to meet them. It's dim, but as I get close, I see one of them is Woodly. He's carrying a big brown envelope.

I stand in front of him. He motions me back. "Let's go inside," he tells me. He touches my shoulder.

My stomach drops and I'm ready to get sick. I hold back the gags and walk. I know a terrible thing is coming.

We go in the house and he motions me to sit on the couch.

"I'm sorry – your boyfriend – he must have given some wrong information about his insulin dose – there were complications." He takes my hand and it disappears inside his big fingers. He looks into my eyes.

I can barely hear his voice, like he's a mile away whispering. "We don't have the report yet, to say exactly what happened. . . ."

I don't hear any words after that, but I see his lips form them. It doesn't matter what he tells me. I know Punch kept his vow.

Woodly puts the thick packet on the table. I can't take my eyes off it.

"Does he have any relatives?" he asks.

"No." I try to look straight at him, get through it so he'll leave.

He says we'll see about the arrangements later. I sign a form and he offers to take me to a friend's house.

"No, thanks." I take a long breath. "I don't want to go anywhere. Just be alone."

He doesn't want to leave me, but I insist. He says he'll call me in a while and send a car if I change my mind.

"I have a car."

I shut the door and pull the phone cord out of the jack. My eyes fill up and I crumple down onto the couch. My grief comes out in shrieks and I don't stop until my throat is raw and all I can do is whine and swallow. I finally open my eyes and see the packet on the table next to me.

I take it and sit up, wipe my eyes so I can see. Inside is Punch's wallet and watch, an envelope, and a lined tablet of writing that reads "The Final Chapter" at the top. Under it is the purple shirt folded perfectly and his underwear and jeans. Punch was able to finish the book and carry out his part of the plan.

I sit on the couch, scared and lonely, and look at the tablet. I never learned to start up the computer, so I can't get the rest of the book. I read what I have.

Punch has used details from our Louie's hold-up and the wild ride to Mallory Dock. We die by gunshot. Punch draws his gun and a cop takes us both down from the side. We splash into the water and sink slowly, "Bloody backs disappearing under the surface of the dark waters, a fitting burial for a man who belonged nowhere on earth, and the woman he loved." I can almost hear music when I read it, and I visualize us, bullet-holed and bloody, but sinking together, never to be apart. I wonder if that's what Punch had intended to happen – our wild ride into the sun and a hail of bullets.

I'm numb and cold when I finish. I don't move from the couch until midnight. By this time we would have done it and been discovered. I think about all the food I was going to eat, and my stomach curdles. I think of how we were going to snuggle against each other. My chest throbs. I can't live by myself. I'm just a miserable walking zombie.

I go into the bathroom and open the medicine cabinet. The sleeping pills are there, the two brown prescription bottles. I reach for them with shaking fingers. I carry them at arm's length into the bedroom. I'm following them into the soft sheets, the ever-after. I'm scared, but I don't have anything to live for. Punch could be somewhere waiting for me – a better place, a better Punch.

My mouth is dry, like I've cried all the moisture out of my body. I go for water in the kitchen. Bill's bowls are still there and the picture of me like Marilyn on the refrigerator. I'm sobbing on the way back to the bedroom. My stomach is an earthquake. I wipe my face with both hands and pull back my hair hard to try to get calm. Our life together had a million terrible minutes, but I'd do anything to have one of them back right now. Nobody ever loved anybody like I loved Punch or he loved me.

I sit shaking on the bed and draw my legs up Indian style. I hold the first bottle of pills and push and turn the lid to open the child safety cap.

I understand Punch's drinking and why he was ready to die. He must have lived in lonely pain most of his life. He didn't want to take a chance on it ever again. I don't either.

I think of my mother, soft and kind, and wonder if I'll follow her gleaming white body into the light like I've heard about on TV. I feel close to her, more peaceful than ever. I close my eyes and pretend that Punch's shoulder is my pillow and Bill's fur is warming my feet. I put an arm around my stomach and hold myself and the baby inside me.

Finally I get the strength to open the bottle and pour the pills into my hand. I stare. Tears run down my face. They aren't pills. They're pastel candy hearts with sayings stamped on. It takes my breath away. I look at each one. Nothing but "I love you's" and "Forever."

I wrench open the second bottle and dump it on the sheets – the same. I picture Punch emptying the little boxes of hearts from the Seven-Eleven, his creamy tan fingers sorting through to find the words he wanted. I wonder if he hid the pills somewhere for himself. My guts are being torn out. I gag and heave. I run to the kitchen sink and feel my stomach bounce, but nothing comes out.

I put my face down on the cool counter. Punch has had the last words even though he's dead. I picture him laughing and shrugging. It would make a good story if he could tell it. But he's dead. I open the silverware drawer. I used the knife once – I can do it again. I know how to slit my wrists, open the veins straight down. I'm Juliette – just like the real Juliet, in that much love and pain. She took a dagger to her heart. I touch blue veins through the thin skin of my arms. That's the spot.

I pull myself up and scoop a handful of hearts into my mouth. I eat Punch's words. They're sweet but dry. I can barely chew them, the only thing they'll find in my stomach, hard evidence of love.

I take out the knife and line the blade up with the long blue vein running down the inside of my wrist. I imbed the point. It's painless compared to my other feelings. A drop oozes out. Pop's "I told you so," comes into my head, his prediction I'd die a bloody death. I stop. I lift the knife and watch the blood well up and run off the side of my wrist. This cutting is crazy. I can't finish it. Punch wanted me to live. Isis will do anything to help me. Pop was wrong.

I put the knife back in the drawer and get a paper towel and press it hard against the puncture. More than me, there's the critter inside, like a tiny hairless Bill. I can't kill it.

27

◆◆◆◆◆◆◆◆◆◆◆◆◆◆◆◆◆

I plug in the phone and call Isis. I don't want to be alone anymore. It rings and rings. Finally she answers. She had just locked her door, ready to drive over.

The rest is a dreamy blur. Isis comes and gets me, takes me home, talks me through the long hours until morning, and then endless days after that, time that almost seems blank now.

A week or so later John, who owns The Island Bookstore, brings me the first eighteen chapters of Punch's manuscript. It was found spiral-bound from the print shop, in alphabetical order on the shelf of Florida writers. A few days later a librarian brings another copy from their stacks. My address is on the front of each for delivery, with identical notes and a "Do-it-Yourself Last Will and Testament" inside. Just like Punch to be sure his work made it into the library and the bookstore.

In the note he asks me to give the book to Albin, who agreed to send it to his publisher friend in New York with all the clippings we saved for publicity. Any money will go to me for chef school – or whatever I want – and to take care of the baby. The loot he was saving under Albin's house was supposed to be mine.

Punch wrote that he realized too late he couldn't set up rules to create life the way he wanted it for us. Something always gets out of control. That's why we need art – the one slim chance humans have at perfection. He expected to get himself shot, go down in glory. He always intended for me to live.

I'm living now – the best I can – for the baby-to-be. Isis and Woodly are my good friends, and I work part-time at the witch shop in return for room and board. At night I write journals about our past. It helps me keep my memories and understand some things about myself. Most days I send Punch a letter. I take it to the dock at sunset, tear it into tiny pieces, and fling it to the breeze where we scattered his ashes. It might be silly, but I don't care.

Moon-cat is back home at Hemingway House, and Bill is my dog. I told the wounded man how sorry I am. He'll be back to work soon. He's kind of a hero in his own mind and doesn't hold anything against me. I pleaded guilty at my arraignment and only got two years probation.

I'm waiting for news about the book, and especially awaiting the day I become a mom. I'm not sure how good life can be without the passion of true love. I miss Punch. The pain is hot and sharp when I think of all of our great times – even most of the worst times. But his world was an impossible place – I couldn't save him. Less madness is starting to sound more interesting.